Assariyah

Assariyah

Money over Everything

La'Toya Makanjuola

Matador
9 Priory Business Park
Wistow Road
Kibworth Beauchamp
Leicester LE8 0RX, UK
Tel: (+44) 116 279 2299
Fax: (+44) 116 279 2277
Email: books@troubador.co.uk
Web: www.troubador.co.uk/matador

ISBN 978 1848768 024

British Library Cataloguing in Publication Data.
A catalogue record for this book is available from the British Library.

Typeset in 11pt Book Anitqua by Troubador Publishing Ltd, Leicester, UK

Matador is an imprint of Troubador Publishing Ltd

Printed and bound in the UK by TJ International, Padstow, Cornwall

MIX
Paper from
responsible sources
FSC
www.fsc.org   FSC® C013056

For all my Grandparents! Mrs Rose Showunmi, Mr Ben Ogunnifa, Mrs Rabi Makanjuola and Prince Oyebamiji Makanjuola. Your legacies live on. I love you all!

ACKNOWLEDGEMENTS

First and foremost I would like to thank the Almighty God for everything he has done for me, for everything he continues to do and for everything that is still to come. Thank you Lord for never letting me go, even though I am not worthy of your love. Thank you for loving me. I love you God! I would also like to thank my wonderful mother and best friend, Juliana Makanjuola. Mummy you mean more than the world to me. Thank you for always believing in me and never saying "I told you so", whenever I messed up! Thank you for being selfless and for all the sacrifices you made for us. You are the definition of SUPERWOMAN! I pray that I'll be half the woman you are someday. I love you always! To my daddy Prince Lekan Makanjuola, gone but never forgotten. I prefer to say L.I.P (Live in peace) because your legacy lives on through all your children. I miss and love you so much Daddy. Thank you to my little big brother, Deji Makanjuola. I'm so very very proud of you. Thanks for reading my drafts and keeping me going. Thank you so much for blessing me with two wonderful and beautiful nephews. Kaleem and Ajani, Auntie's babies! You bring so much joy and happiness into my life. I love y'all more than I love myself! My beautiful darling Anna-Marie I love you sweetie, keep dancing, you are a star! My beautiful Goddaughter, Ty Ty you make me so proud, I love you. Keep shining baby girl! Much love to my girl, my sister friend AsiaChinkyBaby. I see you doll, thanks for gracing my book cover, you look HOTT! I couldn't have done this without your support. I know I drove you crazy making you read chapter after chapter. You are beautiful inside and out, thanks for always having my back. Now let's book that trip to M.I.A! The bills are cleared baby girl. Hahaha we're laughing all the way to the bank! Omar Williams (MeGa) Bay you are my everything! I can't explain this feeling but it is real. As it is written on our tags, "Love is giving someone the power to destroy you but trusting them not to." My love it is yours, I love you always. Thank you for being so real and for always making me laugh, especially when I feel like crying. Special thanks to my sexy chicas, my best friends Kelly Chin and Amoy Chin. My sisters from another mother. Over 15 years of friendship...priceless! Thank you both for always being there for me. Y'all are the best. I love you forever, stay beautiful! My fabulous Evey Eve you are a fighter. I admire your strength. Keep pushing on baby and you will always win. I love you girl! Sometimes Angels walk into your life and leave imprints on your heart, Stefanie you are an angel and I love you doll! Don't change! LuLu you are such a sweetheart! Thank you so much for your help and effort with the photo shoot!

Keep working magic with the brush, you're a fabulous make-up artist! Last but not least I'd like to thank each and every one of you holding a copy of my book (damn it feels so good to say that!) I couldn't have done this without your support so THANK YOU, THANK YOU, THANK YOU! God BLESS you all! I love y'all! Never stop believing, never stop dreaming.

"Belief is definitely paramount in creating your vision but to truly be successful, you must master the art of completion." ~ **La'Toya Makanjuola**

FlawLessDiamondKisses
xxmwahxx

CHAPTER 1

As I sit here contemplating my life, I find myself questioning my very own existence. I'm trying to differentiate the real from the surreal, as everything I have ever known or loved has been ripped apart in a world infected by turmoil and greed. In my world there has always been a thin line between reality and r-e-a-l-i-t-y. You're probably thinking, what the fuck is she talking about? However, before filling you in, let me take you on a journey back down memory lane. You see, in order for you to truly understand, I must take you back to the core of this deep-rooted problem.

It was supposed to be the happiest day of my life. I had longed for this moment since the tender age of five. I always dreamed of having a big Cinderella style wedding and this dream grew bigger with each year that I grew older. Now, at twenty-four, I was getting my fairytale wedding. Everything from the golden horse and carriage, to the ice sculptures of kissing swans and doves at the entrance of the marquee was all I ever wanted. The day had finally arrived and I loved every single moment of it. I walked down the aisle in my butter cream lace Vera Wang gown listening to the sexy voice of Brian McKnight singing 'Back At One'. The lyrics definitely touched a special part of me. It was perfect and totally summarised how I felt. This was for real.

Both of our families and friends were seated in a marquee decorated with gold drapery and jewels, filled with twenty thousand white roses and five thousand vanilla candles. As I walked in, everyone turned around to look at me. They had the look of sheer joy written all over their faces and it took everything in me to fight back the tears. The sensuality and beauty of the venue was surreal, everything was perfect! I looked up the aisle and saw Cameron Simmons smiling at me. The feelings I had for him magnified and, at that moment, I knew that marrying Cameron was the right thing to do. This was the embodiment of my dream.

I couldn't wait till I officially shared his last name. When I reached the top of the aisle, Cameron pulled me close and whispered, "You look beautiful baby." The priest led the ceremony, turning to our family and friends before we declared our vows.

"Does anyone here know any reason why this man and woman should not be joined in holy matrimony? If so, speak now or forever hold your peace."

I stood confidently gazing into Cameron's eyes, surely nothing could go wrong. There was a brief moment of silence. The priest instructed us to repeat after him but before he could lead our vows, I heard a familiar voice coming from the back.

"Hey my name is Assariyah Jones, a cocoa caramel beauty with long, wavy hair. I was the type of girl that every guy wanted on his arm, the one that every bitch loved to hate because she couldn't be me."

My heart froze, this was not happening to me, not today, not in front of my mama, family and friends. Hell No! Out of 365 days in a year, 366 in a leap year, why did this bitch choose to read the pages of my diary on what was supposed to be the happiest moment of my life? I had to do something real quick to stop her from ruining my life.

I yelled out to Jasmina, "Quit playing girl, I'm tryna get married here." She would not quit.

"Marriage, love and loyalty, you don't know the meaning of those words so you don't deserve to be standing there in that ten thousand pounds gown. I won't let you destroy Cameron's life."

Now everyone was looking at her like she was crazy. It was obvious that Cameron and I were meant to be together. By then Cameron was getting pissed off, the priest was looking at me for answers that I did not have and I was trying my very best to remain calm.

"Can someone please just get her out of her; we can clearly see that she is intoxicated."

After I said that, Jasmina kicked off, making her way further up the aisle, "Nah bitch, I'm not drunk, bet you wish I was. See Assariyah I can't leave now, what kind of person would I be if I kept all this juicy info to myself?"

I lunged straight at her in a desperate attempt to

retrieve my diary out of her hands but Vera Wang restricted my movement. She was quicker than I was and moved back freely waving my diary in the air, taunting the hell out of me.

"See I knew you would try that shit," she said.

Cameron stepped in, "Stop Jasmina! You're making a big fool of yourself. Leave now before I throw you out."

Then like a bull let loose Jasmina started screaming, "Cameron you think I'm the fool? Look closely at your bride and you will see that she has been making an even bigger fool of you."

Confusion was written all over his face. Cameron turned to look at me, his frown lines were more prominent than ever. I tried to reason with her before it was too late.

"Please don't do this Jasmina, let us get married and we can talk about this later."

Shaking her head, she pointed at me, "Typical, you always have things your way, well today that shit stops."

Just like that she turned the page she had carefully marked out to destroy my life. I wanted to die as she proceeded to read the venom I had so carelessly written.

I love Cameron I really do, initially I admit it was all about the money and the bling but I have grown to love him. Commitment has always been a shaky area for me but with Cam I couldn't circumvent it. All of a sudden I couldn't wait till I was his wife. However, the thought of sleeping with the same guy for the rest of my life was unfathomable. I figured that if I slept with Tyler one last time before the wedding then I would finally be able to commit to Cam without any regrets. So after a very crazy hen night with my girls and some sexy ass strippers I was feeling horny as fuck from having all those big dicks slapped across my face. I had to go and see Tyler; I called to tell him I was on my way.

I drove like a maniac and within fifteen minutes I was knocking on his door. As soon as he opened up I was blessed with the presence of his half naked body coated in chocolate. He was so cut and defined, 6ft 2" tall with hazel green eyes. Wasting no time he kissed me passionately, sliding one hand under my black v-shaped mini dress. Pushing my French lace knickers to the side he finger fucked my pussy, using his free hand to caress my breasts as he sucked on my erected nipples.

Damn he always knew the right buttons to tweak. My pussy was soaking wet, my juices were creaming all over his hands, my moans intensified. Realising that we were still standing by the doorway, Tyler picked me up, closed the door and placed me on his kitchen counter. Spreading my legs wide open he began to lick my pussy, Ooh aaah shit, his tongue felt so good. I couldn't take it any longer so I grabbed his solid penis and sucked his dick like a lollipop before willing him inside me. Tyler fucked the shit out of me it was crazy. I actually lost count of the times he made me cum.

When she finally stopped reading Cameron turned to look at me with pleading eyes begging for this to be some kind of mistake. I just stood there with tears rolling down my eyes and kept repeating, "I'm so sorry Cam," over and over again. The look in eyes turned stone cold, I had confirmed his worst nightmare.

Kieran his best friend and best man looked at me with utter disdain. He apologised to the guests who were in total shock and asked them to leave.

One by one they began to leave but Cameron invited

them to stay and celebrate with him, "Don't go home, I appreciate you all for coming today, please stay and celebrate the fact that I won't be spending the rest of my life living a big lie with this filthy jezebel. Besides it would be a shame to let all the Beluga caviar, the lobster and champagne go to waste."

The priest was totally out of his element surrounded by so much sin. The sighs and whispering amongst the guests grew louder but truth be told I didn't give a fuck about what they had to say. The only person besides Cam that I felt sorry for was Mama. I had let her down real bad and embarrassed her in front of our family, our friends and a bunch of strangers. My mama was sitting in the front row crying and rocking, my sister Nayla had her arms around her consoling her. I could not forgive myself for the pain and hurt I had caused. I walked towards them trying to obtain eye contact with Mama.

"I'm truly sorry Mama," too ashamed to look at me, she didn't respond to my cry.

"Tell me why Assariyah, why?" Cameron bellowed from behind me.

I felt so pitiful all I could do was keep telling him how sorry I really was.

"Please believe me when I say I never meant to hurt you Cam."

"What a joke, believe you? Bitch you wouldn't know the truth if it slapped you across your fucking face!"

I totally deserved that but I had to get out of there fast.

The whole situation was turning into a complete circus and I was the star attraction. I needed to get out of there, my head was spinning, I felt dizzy, nauseous and faint all at once. If there was ever a moment I wished I could fly, this was it but since I did not possess any super powers I gathered my gown and ran as fast as I could into the Rolls Royce Phantom that awaited Mr and Mrs Simmons.

I was alone, it was not supposed to be this way but I had no one to blame besides myself. After all, due to my selfishness and fear of commitment, I had put myself in this predicament and now I had lost the best thing that had ever happened to me. It is funny how that old cliché, you don't know what you have till it is gone, rings true every single time. How was I supposed to live now? I had nowhere to go. I had grown accustomed to a life of luxury, with Cam I could have and buy anything my heart desired, money was never an issue. Cam's job as the founder and CEO of 'La Chase', an international advertising and marketing agency, meant that he brought home a six-figure salary every month.

The driver finally plucked up the courage to ask me if I was going to be okay. He had been staring at me through his mirror for the majority of the forty-five minute drive in silence, watching the tears roll down my eyes. We were now approaching Cameron's deluxe apartment, situated in the affluent Royal Borough of Kensington and Chelsea. He started by telling me that he could not imagine anyone leaving someone as beautiful as myself and that any man would be lucky to have me, blah, blah, blah.

Why are people automatically programmed to think that the man is always to blame? So fucking stereotypical, I quickly set him straight. "Cam was a good man but I fucked up by sleeping with another guy a week before our wedding and he found out." The skinny ass driver sat there with his mouth open, I hopped out the car without giving him a chance to respond.

Once inside I headed upstairs into our en-suite bathroom, decorated with marble floors and walls encrusted with gold trimmings. I caught my reflection in the mirror and threw up instantly. I was disgusted by the image looking back at me, I wanted to die. I crawled into the built in shower large enough for seven and curled myself into a ball. The automated shower turned on, a sudden blast of cold water came rushing down on me soaking through my gown. I reminisced about the times Cam and I made love in the shower. This was a sure way to catch pneumonia but, at that moment in time, I really could not have cared less.

CHAPTER 2

Cameron and I met each other two years earlier at a party thrown by our mutual friend Jason. The theme of the party was all white, Diddy style. As I swayed my hips from side to side to the beat of Zapp and Roger's 'I Want To Be Your Man', all I could recall thinking was 'DAMN!' There was so much eye candy in the room, the kind that could make a girl catch instant diabetes.

I turned to my girl Jasmina who, at that point, was squeezing the life out of my right arm. I gave her a little squeeze back that was our code for 'I feel you'. Jasmina was gorgeous, she was mixed-race with straight, shoulder length, honey blonde hair. The white gene was unquestionably more dominant, so much so that it made it hard to detect the black in her. Standing at 5 feet 9 inches tall, her slender frame could easily allow her to pass for a model. We were on fire, it was definitely going to be an amazing blazing night.

Jasmina and I decided to pop into the bathroom to

replenish our make-up. There was just way too much hotness in the room to look anything but flawless. After matting out my face with Mac's loose powder, I retouched my lips with my pink Dior lip gloss. I was good to go. My face looked right, my body was banging in my tight, figure hugging, body-con dress. All my curves were on display. At that moment I was grateful for all the extra Pilates sessions I had been attending recently.

I looked hot as hell, it was only right that I made someone's night bright.

"Yo girl, are you ready to bounce?" Jasmina asked.

I had to laugh, Jasmina knew me too well, there was one thing I loved more than men and that was me. I could look at myself all day without getting bored. Some called me vain, maybe I was but I was just appreciating God's creation. After all he had blessed me in the beauty department and to deny that would just be ungrateful.

The party had filled out even more in the last ten minutes that Jasmina and I had been in the bathroom. We went to the bar and ordered double shots of Grey Goose to get us loose. Whilst at the bar I spotted me a hottie. He had to be at least 6ft 2", pure chocolate in complexion and his body was chiseled to perfection. It was clear that he was attracted to me as much as I was to him, we couldn't keep our eyes off each other. After five minutes of flirtatious glances he finally walked over to me.

"You look so beautiful, I just had to come and talk to you."

On that note Jasmina excused herself and told me she

would catch up with me later.

With Jasmina gone, he introduced himself as Tyler.

"Nice to meet you Tyler, I'm Assariyah."

"That's a beautiful name for a beautiful lady."

He was full of compliments that made me blush.

"Flattery will get you everywhere," I said with a slight chuckle.

The conversation between us flowed smoothly, I asked him what he did for a living and he informed me that he was a private fitness instructor.

"Ummm that explains why you are in such a great shape," I stated, feeling on his biceps.

He pointed to my abs with a smile on his face, "I can tell you are a fitness junkie too." I laughed and told him I was far from a fitness junkie but I liked to keep my body looking and feeling tight.

"You know too much jiggling just isn't cute."

We both cracked up laughing and exchanged numbers as he promised to give me a good workout session.

The DJ was on top of his game that night playing all my favourite old skool tracks from 'Push It' by Salt 'n' Pepa to Ghost Town DJ's 'My Boo'.

"Oooh that is my song," I screeched track after track.

Tyler couldn't stop laughing at my random outburst.

"Wanna dance?"

Feeling slightly worried about Jasmina I hesitated before accepting his offer. I guess he could sense my concern because he pointed to Jasmina who was dancing with a guy. I felt relieved knowing that Jas was not alone after all. I took Tyler's hand and led him to the centre of the room and began to gyrate my hips slowly to the beat of the music. This was clearly a turn on for Tyler, I could feel the pressure of his growing manhood against my butt and I cannot even front, I loved the way he felt on me. This was the perfect way to spend my Saturday. I wanted to dance on him all night.

In need of a nicotine fix Tyler wanted to pop outside so he could satisfy his craving. With his profession I was surprised to find out that he was a smoker. I hated the smell of cigarettes and, on a normal day, I would have declined his offer but I decided to go with him. I needed the fresh air anyway, the room was starting to get a little too steamy. He pulled out a packet of Marlboro cigarettes with a lighter shaped in the form of a naked woman. He offered me a cancer stick, shaking my head, I refused. I watched him light his desire and for a brief moment I felt sad. Noticing my mood had changed, Tyler questioned me.

"Hey are you okay?"

"Yeah, I am fine," I replied with a little smile trying to sound convincing but truth be told I was in a dark place right then.

Thoughts of my friend Shelia came to mind. She had only been thirty-five when lung cancer had taken her away from me. She'd always had a frigging stick in her mouth, she smoked no less than fifty a day. I used to tell her that shit would kill her, she would always laugh and say, "Riyah darling, I have to die of something." I felt like crying but fought back my tears to avoid breaking down on Tyler. That shit was too heavy for someone I'd only just met a few hours ago. I had to change things up. I adjusted my thoughts and looked Tyler dead in his eyes.

"You ever thought of quitting?"

"Now and again," he sighed.

I decided it was best not to push him any further.

For the first time that night I realised just how beautiful Tyler really was. The outside light exposed his piercing hazel green eyes, slanted and mysterious. Oh gosh I was in lust. Every time he looked at me with those eyes I had to resist the strong urge to jump on him. All I wanted to do was lick all of that chocolate off his face. Lookswise he was everything I dreamed of and more. Imagine your favourite dessert with extra cream, extra chocolate, extra strawberries, extra caramel, extra cookie dough in your already cookie doughed Ben & Jerry's Ice-cream. Extra! Extra! Extra! That's exactly what I had been blessed with...aaah pure bliss!

"Assariyah, girl there you are. I've been looking for your ass everywhere." I turned to face Jasmina, who was standing behind me with her hands on her hips.

"I'm sorry chica I decided to chill with Tyler whilst he smoked a cigarette real quick."

Throwing me a confused look, she protested, "But you hate the smell of that stuff."

"I know, anyways Jasmina what's up?"

I needed her to stop jumping around the bush and get to the point so that I could turn my full attention back to Tyler.

She pulled my arm gently, "Let me talk to you alone for a minute." I glanced over to Tyler who was puffing away on cancer stick number two.

"Excuse me for a moment Tyler, my girl needs to

have a quick word with me."

"No sweat. I'll be waiting for you," he replied.

I flashed him a smile before walking off with Jasmina. Whatever she had to say had better be real good. When she decided that there was enough distance between us and Tyler she stopped. I thought to myself, what could be so bloody important?

"Okay babe, the thing is I've met this guy called Cameron, he is so buff and…" she paused.

"And…" I pressed her to go on.

"Well he wants us to join him and his friend back at their hotel for a private party." I was completely thrown by her suggestion, that girl had lost her bloody mind.

"Are you mad Jas?"

"Come on girl it will be fun!"

"There is no way I'm following you to chill with two men I don't know, do you not watch the news? Not to mention the fact that I've already met someone who I should really be getting back to now."

As I turned to walk away from Jasmina, she called after me, "Please Assariyah I'm begging you, just do this for me."

I reluctantly agreed to tag along with them but insisted that she gave me a chance to say goodbye to Tyler. I owed him that much. My girl jumped on me giving me the tightest hug, I felt like my ribs were going to break. We walked back together and Jasmina headed back to the party leaving me to handle my business with Tyler.

"Hey Tyler sorry for leaving you like that, I didn't realise I would be gone that long."

"No problem," he assured.

"Now that you're back do you wanna go back and party inside?"

I bit my bottom lip before answering, something I tended to do whenever I got nervous.

"Ummm I would love to but the thing is…"

Before I could finish explaining myself to Tyler, Jasmina and her mini entourage arrived. Tyler looked at the two men standing with Jasmina and then back at me.

"Say no more Assariyah, I totally understand, you're a beautiful lady in high demand, don't let me hold you back."

"It's not what it appears to be Tyler."

"Hey lady, I barely know you so you ain't gotta explain yourself to me."

That was the last thing he said to me before walking away. I was so fucking vexed, I asked the bitch for fifteen minutes to handle my business and the eager beaver was out in five.

One of the men stretched his hand out towards me, "Excuse me miss, I'm Cameron and this is my friend Kieran. I hope we haven't caused you any problems?" Taking a deep breath, I shook his extended hand and kept it short.

"I'm cool thanks."

He smiled, pulling out his Blackberry Bold,

"Well in that case I'll call my driver and have him pick us up."

Less than two minutes had passed and a black Bentley, Continental Flying Spur with personalised plates reading 'La Chase' pulled up beside us. The driver of the car stepped out and greeted his boss.

"Good evening Mr Simmons."

"Hello Derrick, we are heading to The Dorchester."

Derrick greeted us as he opened the doors. The car was sick, red leather interior with a built in DVD entertainment system. Jasmina and I exchanged looks, we both knew what the other was thinking. Damn! Somebody was definitely getting paid!

Once we arrived at The Dorchester I felt like I was in a movie. We were surrounded by grand opulence, the hotel was the epitome of classic beauty. Jasmina had her arms wrapped around Cameron, Kieran and I followed closely behind. Cameron informed the receptionist at the front desk that he had carelessly forgotten his key inside his room. She had her hair styled in a short bob, the red highlights complimented her clear ebony skin and deep brown eyes.

Her name tag read Shaè, she was a pretty girl and looked no older than twenty-one. She flashed Cameron a smile, revealing her pearly white teeth.

"That is no problem Mr Simmons I remember you from earlier, you're staying in the 'Oliver Messel' suite, if my memory serves me correctly."

"That's correct," he said returning the smile, "I promise to look after my key better." Clearly flirting, she placed the new set of keys in his hands.

"No problem, I'm happy to be at your service anytime."

Her blatant disrespect infuriated Jasmina, who gave her, the 'bitch you better back off my man before I whoop your ass' look.

At any other time I probably would have kicked the bitch's ass myself but I was too busy thinking…'WOW! Did she say the 'Oliver Messel' suite?' I had read in several magazines that it had been Elizabeth Taylor's favourite place to stay when she used to visit London. As soon as we entered the room I completely understood why. There was an air of elegance and grace. The art of classical baroque and rococo styles combined together was magnificent. I glanced at Jasmina as she spoke the words that I could not get out.

"This is absolutely beautiful."

I nodded in agreement, the décor had me speechless. My girl was grinning from ear to ear and I couldn't blame her, she had hit the jackpot with Cameron, she really had.

Room service was ordered, lobster, shrimp and champagne, 'oooh wee man this was going to be a fun night', I thought to myself. I no longer felt salty about leaving Tyler, this was so worth it. I could work on getting back into Tyler's good books later. Right then I just wanted to enjoy sipping on Laurent-Pierre Rose. We spent the whole night laughing and getting to know each other better. Jasmina revealed that she was a medical student and they seemed really impressed with her achievements. She always dropped that she was studying medicine when she was trying to upstage me. Unlike her I was still trying to figure out what I wanted to do with my life so I remained quiet on the subject. I felt relieved when Cameron took over the conversation.

Kieran and Cameron had been best friends for ten years. They both shared a passion for business so it was logical for them to enter a business venture together. They decided to start their own advertising and marketing agency about five years ago. For the first three years the company suffered huge losses, the turnover had been pitiful. So bad in fact that Kieran had thought it would be much wiser for them to accept defeat and pack it all in before they lost any more money. However Cameron had refused to give up, the vision he had for 'La Chase' was so strong that he refused to let it go and bought Kieran out instead.

Several months later, 'La Chase' was still losing money, Cameron explained that he was beginning to wonder if he had bitten off more than he could chew. His long break finally came at a huge conference event for various food and household product manufacturers. Offering his services for a quarter of most leading agencies he landed a huge deal with 'Unilever' and ever since then the company's bottom line had been increasing year after year.

I was impressed by his determination and drive but had been left feeling uneasy within myself. Everyone in that room except me had some type of success story to share and I was stuck at first base.

CHAPTER 3

Ring Ring Ring Ring Ring...Ring!

The constant ringing of the house phone was getting on my last nerve. You would have thought that after the fifth ring they would get the hint that nobody was at home. Okay well I was home but not for much longer. I had plans to go shopping with Jasmina but the bitch woke me up around eight, telling me that she was still trying to recover from the last couple of nights that we had been partying and bailed out on me. Never one to miss out on a chance to swipe the cards I decided to go solo.

Ring Ring Ring Ring Ring...Ring!

Who was this lunatic blowing off my phone every five minutes? I had considered pulling the phone out of the socket so that I could get my shit together in peace but changed my mind.

"Hello, who is this?" I asked in an agitated tone, only to be greeted by an automated message from HSBC bank. The bank was chasing me because I had exceeded my overdraft limit. I quickly placed the phone back on the receiver. 'Man I shouldn't have answered the damn phone', I thought to myself. First instincts, when would I learn to stick to mine?

It was time to bounce but not before I completed my daily ritual. A final check in all of the four floor length mirrors in my room. 'WOW…I'm the shit' I mouthed to myself at the sight of my reflection in the mirror. Dressed in a pair of skin tight treggings and a T-shirt I was looking mighty fly, there was no doubt that I had the power to stop traffic. With my medium sized breasts, 26 inch waist, full hips, toned thighs and big round booty, I felt like the term 'cola bottle shape' was invented just for me. Feeling very pleased with my appearance I threw on a pair of classic Louboutin pumps and wrapped my Loro Piana cashmere scarf around my neck to add the finishing touch.

Barely out of my front door and the hollering had already began.

"Yo sexy, slow down ma," a guy called out to me from across the street. He was having a laugh if he thought a girl like me would ever give him the time of day. The funny thing about the situation was that he was actually buff but his dress sense was totally wack. He was rocking skinny jeans with an extra fitted shirt, the only thing that worked was his Prada shoes. I didn't fuck with guys who were in a competition to wear tighter jeans than me. In my eyes they were nothing but dickless cunts with no balls if they could squeeze into that shit. I looked straight past him and kept it moving.

As much as I hated taking it, I opted to go via public

transport rather than calling a cab. I convinced myself that it made more sense, firstly it would be quicker and secondly it was a lot cheaper. Since Jasmina had left me in the lurch I wasn't feeling to break the bank just to get to Bank, where the Royal Exchange was situated. Once I saw the crowd on the platform at Tooting Broadway underground station, I immediately regretted my decision. The Tube was surprisingly overcrowded for a Monday afternoon and it was only 1pm so I hadn't anticipated the rush hour crowd.

The Tube announcements went off, "Please mind the closing doors." I managed to slide myself through the doors just before they fully shut. It was baking hot and the smell in the carriage was overpowering. I took a few deep breaths to avoid passing out. You would have thought that people had never heard of Colgate, Listerine, Sure, plain old soap and fucking water.

To make matters worse the driver kept stopping in the tunnel, a twenty-four minute journey ended up taking frigging forty-eight minutes. Why? All because some stupid loser decided to throw himself in front of a train at Stockwell station. I mean if you wanna kill yourself do it in your own time. When we finally arrived at my stop I was so relieved. I promised myself that would be the last time I ever stepped foot on the Tube again. The Northern Line was bloody diabolical!

My journey had left me feeling sticky and lethargic. I wasn't even in the mood for shopping anymore. I just wanted to freshen up ASAP. Finally inside the Royal Exchange, I walked past a plethora of luxury brands and headed directly for the toilets. I always carried wet wipes with me and pulled them out of my bag to cleanse my face before wiping my underarms. I sprayed Versace Crystal Noir all over myself, immediately releasing notes of gardenia and amber in the room and instantly felt refreshed.

I applied gloss to my lips but didn't re-apply my make-up, after what I had been through I needed my skin to breathe. Not prepared to mix with a big crowd just yet and feeling quite parched I choose to go to the Grand Café. I found a seat and ordered a cup of tea. It felt good being away from the hustle and bustle of the shoppers.

"Assariyah."

I turned around to see who called my name and was taken aback to see Cameron standing behind me. He was about 5ft 11" in height with a medium build. With his light caramel skin and deep smooth waves on his head, he looked good but was not really my type. What were the chances of us bumping into each other a couple of days after we had originally met?

"Hey Cameron, I guess it really is a small world after all," I said, with a smile.

"Actually I've found it is a pretty big world," he replied in jest.

"Haha, so what brings you to the Exchange?" I asked him.

"My office is only a ten minute walk from here so when time permits, I like to take advantage. Let me guess, you're here to shop," he concluded.

"Actually I'm here for tea," I said, pointing to the cup on the table.

"Touché," he said, laughing.

Cameron ordered a drink and sat through thirty minutes of me moaning about the nightmare journey that I had encountered. He empathised with me and encouraged me to go shopping to cheer myself up. I told him that I wasn't really in the mood but would go if he promised to tag along.

He placed his hand on the small of my back pushing me gently, "Let's go," he agreed.

Agent Provocateur was the first stop. I needed some super sexy lingerie. I had plans to get inside Tyler's bed so I needed to be prepared. I hadn't spoken to him since the night I left him at the party but was unable to get him out of my head and was determined to get it on and popping with him. There was so much to choose from in the shop but in the end I opted for the hornette playsuit which was cut out at the waist and hips, leaving very little to the imagination and I loved it. Whilst paying for my new purchase I fantasised about all the freaky positions I wanted to be in. Tyler was definitely getting a call from me that night.

"Damn! Whoever has you in his life is one lucky man and I'd be even luckier if you were my girl." I was surprised by his random outburst.

"Okay Cameron where is this coming from? Shouldn't you be saying this to Jasmina? You know, the girl you hooked up with at the party?" I asked him, frankly.

"No disrespect but forget Jasmina. From the moment I laid eyes on you Assariyah I was drawn by your allure and beauty."

He wasn't making any sense to me. "So why did you go after Jas?" I asked.

He protested, "I didn't, she approached me and started dancing with me. She told me her friend was occupied and pointed you out talking with some dude. I needed a way to get close to you so I seized the opportunity."

I quickened my pace, leaving numerous shops behind this was the last thing I needed.

"Assariyah please slow down," Cameron asked.

I stopped where I was and asked, "All that you said back there, were you being serious?"

"I'm dead serious," he answered.

It was too awkward to look at Cameron so I fixated my eyes on the exclusive diamond collection displayed at De Beers. Hoping to change the subject, I pointed to a pair of champagne cocktail fizz diamond earrings in the window display.

"How beautiful are they?" I said with admiration.

"They would look even more dazzling on you. Just say the words and they are yours."

"Get outta here, you don't even know me and you are offering to buy me diamonds. You can't be for real?" I questioned him in disbelief.

He led us into the store, "I really wish you wouldn't doubt me so much lady."

He signalled for one of the store's advisors to come over to us and told her we wanted the earrings.

"These are one of a kind, your wife has very good taste," she added, politely.

"She sure does." Cameron nodded his head in agreement, before I even had a chance to correct her.

"Why did you let her think I was your wife?"

"Because it's only a matter of time before you are."

Cocky bastard, more fool you, I thought.

"You're crazy Cameron."

"Over you, there is no doubt about that."

I bit my lips and thanked him for the earrings. I still couldn't believe he just dropped over twenty-eight thousand pounds in cash to buy them for me. Shit like that didn't even happen in movies, yet alone to me.

Soon after Cameron asked Derrick to drop him back to his office and to make sure that I got home safely. He placed a kiss on my forehead.

"Make sure you call me, beautiful," he said, getting out of the car.

"I don't have your number," I replied slightly confused.

"When you get home look inside the pocket of the blazer you wore at Jason's party, I slipped my card in there."

I called Jasmina as soon as I got home.

"Babe you'll never guess what just happened to me."

"What? Tell me quick girl," she quizzed excitedly.

I told her everything that went down with Cameron from us drinking tea to shopping and best of all about the diamond earrings he bought me. I knew she would be slightly touchy but her reaction was unexpected.

"What the fuck, have you lost your fucking mind?" she hollered through the phone. I didn't understand why she was getting all hot and bothered, so I tried to make her see sense.

"Calm down Jas, it ain't that serious, what are you flipping for?"

"Ain't that serious, don't give me that Assariyah. You knew how much I liked him and then you have the audacity to call me and flaunt the shit all up in my face. Why couldn't you just leave him to me? I mean you can have any guy you want."

Man this girl was tripping over a dude she had known for forty-eight hours.

"He is not even your fucking type," she continued to rant.

"Well the size of his pocketbook is so my type."

"You make me sick," Jasmina growled at me.

She was really pushing my buttons so I flipped on her.

"Quit bitching, dude ain't feeling you like that. He wants me. He told me so himself. So tell me what's the point in letting all that money go to waste?"

I paused for a minute or so waiting for Jasmina to respond. I could barely hear her breathing, nothing but silence travelled through the receiver. Finally she was beginning to see things from my point of view, I knew she would eventually.

I switched up the tone of my voice, making sure I sounded bubblier before addressing her again. "Tell me what you want and next time I'm with him I'll pick it up for you. I know you've been wanting that Louis V bag, the sleek Monogram Vernis one in red for the longest!"

"You know what?"

"What?" I asked her anxiously, only to be greeted by the sound of Jasmina kissing her teeth.

"F-U-C-K Y-O-U Bitch!" she spat out and slammed down the phone.

Oh my gosh, I know this chick didn't just end the conversation like that. I gripped the phone tightly, fuming inside. Like why couldn't she just work with me? Dude was loaded and we could milk him for days but no she wanted to act all dumb and catch feelings over a guy who wasn't even feeling her. Well I tried to be nice but fuck it. I'm going to make sure I get mine from that nigga.

I swore to myself that I'd never mess with any guy who didn't have his paper stacked after the shit that loser Sammi put me through. At the time Sammi and I had been dating for about four months. It was Valentine's Day and I was more than thrilled when he told me he wanted me to be his official girl. He arrived at my house looking all sexy dressed in an all black Adidas tracksuit and fresh white Jays. His mocha skin drove me crazy and he had his hair out just the way I liked it. I loved running my fingers through his wild coolie hair when he left it unbraided.

I planted a deep, passionate kiss on his full lips to thank him for the blue roses he had bought for me. They were so enchanting, roses were my favourite, especially the blue ones and I was touched that he'd remembered. I took his hand and led him to the balcony where the candlelit dinner I'd prepared awaited. I hated cooking so, on the rare occasions that I decided to throw on an apron and get my Delia Smith on, you had to know that I was feeling you big time.

The noises Sammi was making whilst he ate the

honey-soy broiled salmon I had prepared reassured me that I'd done a good job. After the main course I left the table to get dessert, profiteroles filled with cream, covered in chocolate sauce. Approaching the table on my way back I nearly dropped the dessert bowls I was holding when my eyes caught sight of the Tiffany & Co bag on the table. No fucking way! I adored Tiffany's. My, my, my…this was turning out to be the best Valentine's Day yet.

I sat down eagerly and rummaged through the bag, it had two boxes inside. I smiled so much that my cheeks ached. When my hands eventually stopped shaking, I unwrapped the white ribbon tied neatly on the box. He had bought me a sterling silver necklace with a matching bracelet. I was so chuffed.

I climbed on top of him to show my appreciation. He bit and sucked on my neck as I straddled him. Sammi held on to my hips and bounced me up and down in full force on his solid dick. The thickness of his rock compensated for the couple of inches he had lacked in length. His penis stretched my walls in all directions, at the time it had felt like I was being ripped apart but it was so pleasurable. I moaned deeply in between the mixture of ecstasy and pain he put my aching body through. I had venerated his dick, it was too much.

"Whose pussy is this?" I remembered him asking as he continued to bounce me up and down.

"It's mine," I answered him defiantly, feeling brave. That had been a big, big mistake! He lifted himself, making sure he was still inside me and placed me at the tip of the table. Holding both of my legs over his head, he pounded my pussy, each pump was harder and longer than the last one.

"Ummm ahhh…oooh…shit…shit Sammi it's yours." I had cried out but he didn't stop until his body began to shake and he had released a load of cum inside me. He pulled out of me but he was nowhere near finished, he meant business.

Moving in slow circular motions, he flicked my clit with his fingers, pinching them slightly. This caused a whole other sensation that had me jerking back and forth vigorously. Just when I felt like I couldn't take anymore, he went in for the kill and stuck his tongue deep inside my pussy lapping up all my love juices, whilst slowing kneading my asshole. I came with a force, shaking uncontrollably and before I knew it I had fallen into a deep sleep.

The next morning when I woke up I found myself in the bedroom. Sammi must have carried me in because I couldn't remember walking in there myself. I called out for him but there was no answer. He had already left but I wasn't mad. The performance he had laid down the night before was enough to keep me going for at least a week and that was a long time considering how much I loved to fuck! Stretching all the way to the balcony, my pussy still ached. I had left my gift out in the balcony and couldn't wait to try them on but I noticed something that I hadn't spotted the previous night. The colour of the boxes looked a shade darker than that of the distinctive turquoise blue associated with Tiffany and Co. No way! I thought to myself, shaking out the doubts that it was fake. He wouldn't, I mean who does that? I had to find out, I needed to be absolutely sure, so I took the package and the jewellery he had given me to Selfridges in New Bond Street.

My heart pounded as I headed towards Tiffany's concession. It's real, it's real, I repeated to myself. Maybe they had changed it slightly, you know, a Valentine's special edition or something, it was possible after all. The store was quite busy and, with it being fairly small, I could see everything. I spotted an Arab couple admiring engagement rings, they looked crazily in love. I was the only black person in the store at the time and waited nervously for assistance.

A middle aged man with salt and pepper hair came over to me when he was free. "Hello, how can I help you?" His accent gave away that he was of French origin. He led me to the counter and I pulled the gift Sammi had given me out of my bag. He immediately raised an eyebrow but didn't say anything until I opened one of the boxes.

"This is not a Tiffany piece," he fired back abruptly.

I was beyond embarrassed, all eyes were on me.

"Are you sure?"

Looking back I realised I shouldn't have asked him again as I just drew more attention to myself but I had wanted him to tell me so badly that he had made a mistake.

"Yes this is definitely not one of ours, look at the box, it does not have the colour of Tiffany blue," he said, as he held out the original.

Words cannot even describe how small and low I had felt as I hurried out the store. I had been twenty then but every time I thought about that incident the wound was still as raw as the first time, it cut deep.

I needed to release my anger, writing was my therapy. I picked up my diary and began to vent. Money over everything! That was my state of mind. The pages of my diary knew me better than anyone. My diary never spoke back and thus never judged me.

CHAPTER 4

I arrived at Tyler's home as arranged. He was stunned when I told him that I was coming to see him after 11pm but, to my relief he agreed nonetheless. I needed to feel him now more than ever, especially after the argument with Jasmina I had to release some tension. It didn't take me long to get ready. I had a quick shower, pulled my hair back in a messy chignon and threw on the hornette playsuit I had purchased earlier on that day. My body was lightly scented with Victoria Secret's 'Love Spell' body butter. I didn't want to go overboard by spraying perfume because if things went my way, like they usually did, there would be a lot of licking and sucking. The last thing he needed was the taste of perfume in his mouth. Tonight I would bless him with my natural scent and leave the taste of my juices lingering on his tongue.

Personally I did not see the point in wasting time. I mean why spend several months dining out, watching movies, endless late nights staying up and talking on the phone, all for one ultimate result? The pussy or the dick depending on whose perspective you wanted to look at it from. I knew what I wanted so simply cut out all the bullshit in between.

"Damn Ma!" Tyler said, licking his lips. "All this for me?"

Standing with my legs slightly apart, I opened my Mac coat even wider to give him more of an eyeful.

"Well you did promise to give me a good workout session, show me what you got," I challenged him seductively.

He looked at me intensively. "I'll be right back," Tyler informed me.

He disappeared into another room and left me and my throbbing pussy standing in his living room for what felt like forever and a day. In actual fact, he was in and out in less than two minutes.

"Hey lady, put this on."

I was baffled by his actions but I took the XXL white shirt he had stretched out to me and reluctantly put it on as he ordered.

"Okay so what is this all about?" I asked him unenthusiastically.

"We're going for a walk and I don't want your half naked butt to freeze to death."

"A walk!" I exclaimed, pointing to my six-inch stilettos. "If you haven't noticed these shoes were not made for walking!"

"Don't worry it's not that far," Tyler said, grabbing my hands gently.

"Nuh-huh I'm not going... Oh my gosh, put me down Tyler," I screamed as he scooped me up in his arms, pressing my chest against his hard body.

"Stop fidgeting woman or I'll make you walk," he said playfully.

Giving in, I threw my hands up.

"This better be good Tyler."

"Trust me," he replied.

My nipples grew even harder upon contact with Tyler. My pussy was dripping to the point that I could feel my thighs getting sticky. I needed to be fucked so badly at that moment but I was left without any wood inside me. 'Trust me'. I replayed his words over in my mind. I was beginning to doubt the fact that he was even straight. Seriously what red-blooded heterosexual male goes out of his way to cover up a half-naked woman, mind you, not just any naked woman but moi, the crème de la crème? Nah this dude was either fruity or he did not live alone because this shit just didn't make any sense to me. On the drive over to his all I could picture was Tyler ripping off what little lingerie I was wearing and having his wicked way with me but here I was going for a walk.

Ten minutes later we were standing outside of a fitness centre.

"Here we are," Tyler said letting me down.

Now I was even more confused, what the fuck is he bringing me here for?

"I work here," he announced, as if he were reading my thoughts.

"I promised to give you a good workout session remember?"

Pulling out a set of keys from his pocket he opened

up the doors, triggering off the alarm system. Tyler rushed to the back to switch off the alarm before offering to give me a tour of the facilities.

I felt mentally and sexually frustrated, time was the last thing I wanted to waste. "What are we doing here exactly?" I asked him, sounding more impatient than I perhaps would have liked to come across.

"Calm down ma, when you called at 11pm to tell me you were coming over I figured you were mine for the night so relax and let me show you around."

Aaargggh! This guy was driving me up the wall. I swear down he is lucky he looks as sexy as he does because if he had been anybody else I would have left the moment he handed me his stupid shirt. Come on Assariyah breathe...breathe...breathe. Think before you speak, "So what do you have in mind Tyler?"

"Ummm I could tell you but I'd much rather show you," he said rubbing on my shoulders.

He led me to a room that smelled of aromatherapy oils.

"Get naked and lie face down on one of these tables." I peeled the shirt I was wearing off slowly, leaving my hornette playsuit on but that was not enough for him.

"Take it all off, ma." I did as I had been told and got completely naked. My heart pounded heavily as I approached the massage table he was standing by. He fucked me mentally with his eyes, turning me on even more than I already was.

I laid face down on my stomach and immediately felt Tyler's strong hands on my back. He began by massaging my shoulders and worked his way down my back, he brushed his hands against my butt and started from the top again. He made me feel so sensual, our pheromones travelled through the air increasing our desires for each other. In all my life I couldn't recall ever wanting or needing a guy as much as I wanted Tyler at that point in time.

"Fuck me Tyler," I begged him, but he continued to massage me, rubbing in between my thighs evading my pussy, which I wanted him to so badly touch.

I was beyond wet, my pussy had created a rainfall, it was in its very own monsoon season. I was sure that Tyler could feel my juices on his hands. He turned me over slowly, admiring my naked body, he was fucking me mentally again but I wanted him to fuck me physically and all this teasing was becoming unbearable.

I couldn't hold out any longer so I reached for his belt buckle but he grabbed my hands stopping me in my tracks.

"Follow my lead ma." I nodded my head and we ended up in the sauna room. Tyler took off his shirt and pulled down his jeans leaving just his crispy white boxers on. Our bodies perspired copiously as the heat in the sauna increased. Tyler removed his boxers and I had to stop myself from drooling. His naked body looked so delectable wet and I knew he would taste even more delicious. I was totally hot for him and wanted to reach for him so badly, but he had already made it clear that he was in charge.

"This is so relaxing, don't you just love a good session in the sauna?" he asked me.

"Yeah this is nice," I agreed with him but 'touch me, kiss me, fuck me' were the only words circulating in my mind and my body was dying to scream them out. I crossed and uncrossed my legs more times than I could recall. Being in the same room and not having any contact with him was too dangerous for me. I was not used to having to wait for shit. I needed to feel him, I wanted him to show me and give me everything he had.

Fuck it! If he wouldn't touch me I'd do the shit myself. So I began to rub my nipples, he sat back to watch me and smiled but didn't say a word. I positioned my body so that I was directly in his view. My legs were spread wide open and I made sure I locked eye contact with him before inserting two fingers in my honey pot. A soft moan escaped my lips as I worked myself and built up a rhythm, it felt good and I continued to finger myself with pleasure.

Tyler was enjoying my mini peep show, his penis was getting hard and rising right before my eyes. He signalled for me to come over to him and patted his lap for me to sit on it. Then he grabbed my face and pressed his lips against mine, he kissed me like I had never been kissed before.

Ummmmm this is more like it I thought.

"You're so fucking sexy," he said slapping my butt before pushing me down on his penis.

"Aaaaah shit," I moaned, not believing that this was actually happening. His dick was extremely thick and long, he was really big so I found it a bit hard accommodating his full length. I moved around slowly, taking a little more of him in each time I bounced up and down on his meat. I was having sex with the sexiest guy I had ever met in a sauna. It hurt like hell but felt so good.

"Assariyah, you okay ma?"

"Ooohhh yeah…yeah I'm okay."

He held my arms back whilst penetrating me from behind to prevent me from using them to push him away when he went in too deep. My whole body was on fire but this was the best kind of pleasure I had felt in forever and I didn't want it to stop.

The heat in the sauna had become too much to bear and we both needed some air. Tyler picked me up and carried me over to the shower area. He switched the shower on and as the cold water fell and cooled down our bodies, Tyler turned things up a notch. Whilst standing he flipped me upside down in the 69 position. My pussy was in his mouth and he began to vibrate his tongue on my clit. He made me feel real good so it was only fair that I returned the favour. I took his dick in my mouth and sucked on it the best I could in the position I was in. At first I was gagging but the more I relaxed my throat the less I choked on his cock.

An hour had passed and we were still going at it. We went from the sauna to the shower and finally in the Jacuzzi. The pressure from the bubbles in the Jacuzzi against my clit and Tyler fucking me doubled the intensity of the pleasure I was feeling. I moaned really loudly at first, then softly and then eventually I felt too weak to utter a sound but my body would not stop shaking. I could feel Tyler coming as he grabbed on to my hips and pushed his penis even deeper inside me. I was coming at the same time, he was too much for me. He fastened up his pace and fucked me hard real fast. He pulled out of me and I allowed him to enter my warm mouth. I sucked him off until he began to jerk and he squirted his cum all over my face.

From that day on I became hooked to Tyler and his dick, we were literally inseparable. We had an agreement that worked for us. It was great sex, nothing more, nothing less. Whenever he needed me I was there and when I needed him he was there, no questions asked.

Tyler made me feel so alive. He was never afraid to try anything new and opened my eyes up to a whole other world sexually. Tyler was a wild beast that couldn't be tamed. When he put it on me, he made me hit octaves that would give Mariah Carey a run for her money.

While Tyler wanted my body, Cameron wanted all of me, he wanted to know every inch of my soul and that scared me. With Tyler I wasn't afraid of getting hurt, like I said it was just sex. Cameron was after love and I wasn't very good at sharing my heart but, no matter how hard I tried to push Cameron away, he refused to budge. He had fresh flowers and gifts delivered to my house almost every day for two weeks until I agreed to go on a date with him and for our first date he had flown me out to Paris for dinner at the Eiffel Tower. That was just the kind of sweet guy Cameron was and any lady in her right mind would have appreciated and cherished him but I had been stupid and clung on to the comfort of casual sex with Tyler instead of being faithful to Cameron, and it had cost me everything.

CHAPTER 5

My alarm clock had been driving me crazy all morning, after hitting the snooze button for the fifth time I finally managed to switch the bloody thing off and drag myself out of bed. I had an appointment at Camden that I couldn't afford to miss.

Camden Town was one of my favourite places for two reasons. The first reason being that it was where my hairdresser Akin Konizi, the creative genius behind Hobs Salon worked his magic on my hair. Secondly it was the home of Gilgamesh one of the best Pan-Asian restaurants in the whole world. The food was absolutely divine and with the combination of the interior's exotic imagery, Gilgamesh was a true glamorous affair to be experienced by all at least once.

I pulled out of Jamestown Road feeling brand new, with my new fringe I could hardly recognise myself. I looked sexier and edgier than I had looked in a while. My attitude towards my appearance had become some what blasé after the wedding so much so that I was letting myself go. I knew I had to fix up fast when I put a comb through my hair and a huge chunk came out. That was the wake-up call I needed to get my shit together and I couldn't think of anyone better than Akin Konizi to make my hair fabulous again. The cut set me back around six-hundred and fifty pounds with treatment but it was so worth it. I was feeling myself again, the weather in London was sunny for a change so I dropped the top of my red Porsche, turned up the radio and let Carrera do her work.

I was heading towards St. Pancras Road driving at a speed of no more than forty miles per hour when I saw the police car flashing its emergency lights for me to pull over. Fuck! I so didn't need this right now. A bald man of stocky build dressed in uniform walked over to the side of my car. His partner, who looked a lot younger and was taller and leaner stood by the passenger side. As one of my girls once told me, the police were nothing more than a bunch of crackers dressed in fancy dress costumes. I hated the fucking police.

The stocky one did all the talking.

"Good afternoon m'am please produce your driver's licence and insurance certificate." This had to be some type of joke I thought to myself while looking through my glove compartment and handed over my licence. I couldn't find the insurance certificate but I was legit so I didn't have to worry about shit. Well that's what I thought until the officer started treating me like a criminal.

"M'am place both your hands on the steering wheel

where I can see them, now step out of the car with your hands over your head."

"You can't be serious?" I asked, shaking my head in disbelief. "I haven't done anything wrong."

"I'm afraid it is quite the contrary. This vehicle has been reported stolen, according to my records you are not the registered owner of the car and to top it all off you have no insurance cover."

"What the hell do you mean stolen? This is my damn car."

"I need you to watch your language m'am," he said, sternly.

"Look I'm sorry okay but you threw me off guard. This is my car and it has been for the last year. My husband…I mean ex-fiancé bought it for me as a gift."

"Ex-fiancé huh, what's his name?" he asked, while rubbing his beard.

"His name is Cameron Simmons."

I could tell from the expression on his face that he didn't believe a word I was saying but I was telling the truth.

"Well that's quite funny because a Mr Simmons reported the vehicle stolen. You have the right to remain silent. Anything you do say can and will be used against you in a court of law. You have the right to a solicitor. If you cannot afford a solicitor, one will be appointed to you. Do you understand these rights as they have been read to you?"

I was in shock and could only manage to nod my head.

I had never been in trouble with the law and the

thought of sitting in a grimy cell made me cringe. The handcuffs on my wrists felt so uncomfortable and they were not even put on as tightly as they could have been. I can't believe Cam would even do this shit. It had been six weeks since the wedding. I had driven this shit countless times since then so why would he wait until now to pull this mess?

During the ride back to the police station I explained the situation at least three times to the arresting officer, PC Monroe, but he insisted that they were just doing their job and had no choice but to take me in.

"This is totally unnecessary," I said, weeping as he closed the doors of the cell on me.

"Are you sure you do not want a solicitor?" he asked me once again.

"What for? I keep telling you that I haven't done anything wrong."

He remained silent and turned to walk away. I heard the sound of his footsteps getting further away and buried my face in my hands. I didn't belong here in this hell hole.

Two hours had passed and I was still locked up in a cell. I couldn't believe that people actually lived this way. The cell could not have been any bigger than six by eight feet in size and reeked from the toilet being in the same space, it was totally inhumane. I cannot describe the huge relief I felt when I heard the keys turning in the keyhole.

I ran to the door, "Am I free to go?"

"I'm afraid not lady, the owner of the car has been informed about the status of the vehicle and he insists on pressing charges."

I wanted to scream but what good would it have done?

"The interview room is ready, have you reconsidered about having some representation?"

"Nah I'm good," I replied.

I could tell that the officer was beginning to feel sorry for me but he had a job to do and was just following the procedures.

Another officer was already waiting inside the interview room. PC Monroe introduced him as PC Mack. After several hours of interrogation they let me go with a caution, three points on my licence and a fine for supposedly not having insurance. It came to light that although Cameron had bought me the car as a gift, I never really owned it. The shit had been in his name all along. I was insured as a second driver but he had removed my name, leaving me uninsured about two weeks prior to the arrest.

Six hours later and I was finally released. I collected my bag and other belongings at the reception and waited for the cab that they had called for me. As I sat waiting anxiously I took a look in my compact Chanel mirror, closing it just as quickly as I had opened it. My eyes were red and puffy from all the crying I had been doing. I went from looking and feeling fabulous to looking like a hot ass mess.

Beep Beep Beep! I figured my cab had arrived from the sound of the horn outside but waited for one of the officers to confirm that it was indeed for me. It hadn't actually registered in my brain until then that my baby had been divested from me. Damn I loved my car and, except for my jewels, it was the only asset I had left with any real value. I had banked on using it as a back-up plan if times got hard. I could simply sell it and use the proceeds to get by till I was back on my feet. That plan was now out the window.

I was glad to be out but walked towards the run down Ford Fiesta feeling totally unimpressed. A few hours earlier I was riding in a fucking Porsche convertible and now I had to sit in a Fiesta. I wasn't sure which was worse being locked up or being seen in that car. They could have sent a half decent car like a Volkswagen Golf. This was not the one, I mean my bloody bag cost more than this shit.

"Where to lady?" the cab driver enquired.

"I'm staying at the Marriott Hotel in Park Lane." He started to type the address into his Tom Tom but stopped to ask me for the post code. Luckily I dropped a few of the hotel's cards in my purse upon arrival. I searched through it and handed him a card. I wasn't in a talkative mood, I just needed silence to clear my thoughts and figure out what my next move would be but this driver could talk for England. Question after question poured out of his mouth, "What happened to you lady? You sure don't look like the criminal type, how did you end up there?"

"Man will you just shut the fuck up and drive like you are being paid to do. While you are at it, change direction and head towards Chelsea."

CHAPTER 6

It felt really strange standing outside Cameron's apartment. Not too long ago this was my home and we had shared many happy memories here together. Now, instead of using my set of keys to enter the property through the private area, I had to wait for security to give me clearance via the visitor's gate. I pushed the buzzer and waited anxiously for a response.

"Good evening, please state your name and who you are here to visit."

I was familiar with most of the security but did not recognise the voice behind the intercom, so I figured that he had to be new. Should I? Should I not? I contemplated lying about my name to avoid being denied entry just in case Cameron had given instructions to his security team not to allow me into his residence.

"Please state your name." The voice came through the intercom again. Fuck it! I thought. No more lies, deceit was the reason I was in this mess right now.

"Hello, my name is Assariyah, I'm here to see Cameron."

To my delight the lights on the intercom flashed green and the electric gates opened up slowly.

I had been praying for an opportunity to see Cameron and discuss things through but it had never happened. I called several times to speak to him on the phone but he only answered my call once and told me never to dial his number again. After that conversation, every other time I tried to call my calls were diverted straight to voicemail. I had so much to say but now that I was standing right before him I did not know where to begin. Eyes that were once filled with love and adoration for me stared at me vehemently with nothing but disdain.

"Hello Cameron, I really need to talk to you. Do you mind if I come in?" I found the courage to ask him.

"Whatever you need to say, you can say it out here and make it quick because, frankly, I've got more important things to do with my time," he said, coldly.

I knew this wasn't going to be easy but he was making it extremely hard for me. I didn't feel comfortable talking to him on the stairs with the security guards wandering around the compound. I pleaded with him to let me in.

"Cam please, all I'm asking for is ten minutes of your time, I really need to talk to you inside."

"That's ten minutes of my life that I'll never get back, I have no time left to spare for you."

"Stop! Please wait," I cried as he turned to leave. "I just need ten minutes, please."

He stopped, "You have five minutes."

Once I was inside I noticed that all my portraits in the hallway had been removed, it was to be expected but I was still hurt. Deep down in my heart I was still hoping for a reconciliation with Cam but he had already started erasing me from his life. He saw me staring at the barren walls.

"You now have four minutes," he said, in a frosty tone.

"Please don't be like that Cameron."

"Three minutes."

"Okay." I took a deep breath before proceeding, "You had me arrested, why?"

"You had something of mine," he replied, nonchalantly.

"You bought that car for me Cameron, what do you mean?"

"No correction I bought that car for my fiancée, my wife and you are neither one, you are nothing to me."

His words cut deep, my defences were down. "You could have just called me Cam, I would have brought the car back."

"Quit calling me Cam. To be honest Assariyah, I don't have shit to say to you. Being in your presence makes me sick. I loved you, my love was real but it wasn't enough for you."

"Cam, sorry Cameron, I understand that you are angry with me but I need you to know that I never meant to hurt you."

"The last two years of my life has been nothing but a complete lie. You humiliated me in front of my family, friends and business associates and now you have the audacity to walk in here like I owe you shit. Never meant to hurt me… huh," he fired, sarcastically.

"Please find it in your heart to forgive me. My life is so incomplete without you. I love you Cam," I replied with tears streaming down my face.

He blew up at me losing control. "Look your tears don't mean shit to me, the words 'I love you' doesn't mean anything coming from you. Now get the fuck outta here before I throw you out."

"Please give me a second chance Cam, I swear things will be different," I begged him, earnestly.

"You're a pathetic excuse for a woman, why don't you go back to your lover so he can tweak all the right buttons?" He punched the wall out of rage before turning to walk away from me.

I couldn't just let him walk out of my life. Crying hysterically, I dropped to my knees and grabbed on to his leg in a desperate attempt to stop him from leaving me.

"Cameron I love you," I screamed.

"That's too bad because I fucking hate you bitch," he replied, shaking me off in disgust.

He ran upstairs leaving me looking pitiful on the floor. My pride was non-existent but I didn't care because I needed him back in my life.

A few minutes later he was standing at the top of the stairway throwing things at me. Dresses by Azzedine Alaïa, shoes by Christian Louboutin, bags by Hermès and Louis Vuitton cases all came flying at me, one after the other.

"Take your shit and leave before I call security to throw you out."

"Cameron please don't, I need you."

"I hope Hermès keeps you warm at night, we both know that's all you really care about, gold digging whore."

"That's not true Cam."

"Bullshit! Six weeks, it has been six whole weeks Assariyah and not once did you stop by."

"That is not fair Cameron and you know it. I called you over and over again but you refused to answer any of my calls."

"Oh I see but the moment your precious Porsche gets taken away here you are knocking at my door. Just when I think you can't get any worse you still manage to amaze me." With that he pushed a buzzer to alert his security team, they rushed in within seconds and, upon their arrival, he ordered them to remove me and my belongings off his premises.

Back at the hotel that night I was too heartbroken to sleep. I laid on the bed weighing my options. Cameron did not want anything to do with me. I was too ashamed to go back to my mama. Nayla had the twins and her husband to look after. Besides I could not stand her husband and I refused to give them the satisfaction of seeing me so vulnerable. I could not afford to keep paying the hotel rate of three-hundred and fifty pounds a night.

My funds were running super low, I had one-thousand pounds left in cash and, once that ran out, I'd be totally broke. I was in need of serious money and I needed it fast. Cameron had always provided everything I needed, he gave me his credit cards plus a weekly allowance but I was always buying shit straight off the catwalk before it even reached the stores. I had clothes worth thousands of pounds in my Louis suitcases but I was on the verge of homelessness. I realised how frivolous I had been with my finances. Not once did I ever think of saving for a rainy day.

I decided that, first and foremost, I would downgrade to one of those cheap hotels but even at a rate of seventy-nine pounds that would only buy me ten nights or so off the streets because I still needed food. I racked my brain thinking of ways to make money, that's when it hit me. I looked down at the rock that glistened on my ring finger and decided to pawn it.

The next day I followed through with my plan and visited a pawnbroker. I handed my ring to a medium-sized man in his early forties. He gave it the once over using a magnifying glass to examine the gem for flaws. "I'll give you five-thousand for it," he said, rubbing his chin.

"Are you crazy?" I asked him in shock.

My engagement ring was worth ten times that. His offer was a kick in the teeth, there was no way I was selling it for that price, no fucking way. It was daylight robbery, I was desperate but I was no sucker. I walked out the store in distress. I did not know what else to do.

I had never even had a job before, where would I start with no experience or reference. I mean how was I supposed to function? I was not like those regular bitches. I couldn't imagine being stuck in an average job for peanuts. I looked too good to stand behind a counter selling things to people. I was the one that bought out the store. I was used to being spoilt. I could not see myself working but it was time to get real or I wouldn't survive.

CHAPTER 7

Many people often think 'selling your soul' involves rituals to the devil, drinking human blood from a cup, allegiance to the Freemasons or Illuminati but it can be something much smaller than that. The moment you begin to compromise your morals and values for worldly goods that is the act of selling your soul. In my case not only was I selling my soul but I resulted to selling my body to the highest bidder. I had a lifestyle to maintain, an insatiable taste for luxury that the regular nine to five job failed to satisfy. I mean what kind of fool do I look like to slave away for eight hours a day only to bring in less than two hundred and fifty pounds a week after the leeches in the form of the Government took their taxes? So I decided to join Precision Escorts. Precision only dealt with the most elite clientele and the rates offered were much higher than standard escorts agencies.

It was never my intention to sleep with men in the beginning but after calling several agencies and receiving the same information, I soon found out the idea that I had in my mind of escorts accompanying men solely to dine out simply did not exist. I learned fairly quickly that dinner dates were fine as long as dessert came in the form of my pussy served on a platter.

Isabella Von Tini, the owner of Precision, asked me to send a profile picture and a full body shot. If she liked what she saw, she would give me a call to arrange a face to face meeting.

"We only hire the most stunning girls to join our family. Like all goods you invest in, you have to see it to know its value." She spoke calmly and softly, placing emphasis on stunning, invest and value. She had turned me into a commodity in less than two minutes. I had doubts but had to push them aside.

I emailed her a couple of shots from my phone. Money talks and bullshit walks so I had to comply. My iPhone rang thirty minutes later, Isabella Von Tini's named flashed across my screen. I knew the bitch would call. My face was beautiful, my body was insane, she would have been a fool not to call.

She wanted to see me as soon as possible and asked if I would be able to come down and visit their office later on that day. I hadn't expected things to move so quickly but I guess, as Isabella rightfully put it, "Time is money and time waits for no one."

"First impressions last forever, so captivate them at the beginning and you'll be successful," she advised. "We look after our girls here. Our drivers pick you up and drop you back to ensure your safety." She went on to say, "If you need somewhere to stay we have newly built apartments that some of the girls share and stay in. The money is good here so you don't have to worry about keeping up with payments."

Wow, I had to give this woman her props not only was she making money from whoring us out but she wanted to play landlady as well.

The jewels draped around her neck already spoke a thousand words. She was swimming in money off men swimming in girls like me. I did need somewhere to stay, I only had seven more days left at the Travel Lodge, but I was not about to give her control over my whole life. On top of that I hated sharing my personal space with strangers, I had too much expensive shit and I couldn't trust any of those bitches. I didn't feel a way to kick a basic bitch's ass but that was drama I didn't want or need so it was best to avoid it. My mama always said that prevention is better than cure. I declined Isabella's offer and could hear the disappointment in her voice.

"Well if you change your mind, let me know."

"Will do," I replied, but my mind was already made up.

Now all I had to do was wait for Isabella to come through with my first job.

Over the next few days I was very particular about what I ate and exercised like crazy. It helped to pass time and took my mind off a few things. I still hadn't heard from Isabella and my time at the hotel was running out. I was on the verge of dialling her number when my phone rang.

"Hi Rose, it's Isabella, I hope you are free tonight because I have a job for you."

I wanted to scream, 'yes yes yes I'm free' but

composed myself before answering. "Let me check my diary real quick," I said, trying to make myself seem busier than I actually was. "I'm free Isabella."

"Fabulous," Isabella replied and proceeded to give me the brief for the job.

I listened attentively and took down the details.

"Have you got all that Rose?" she asked, with a sense of urgency in her voice.

"Dino will pick me up at seven o'clock. Dinner at Nobu in Berkeley street for eight o'clock, reservation is under the name Tim Bakhtin. Tim will hand me a brown envelope, count the cash in the bathroom. No envelope, no date, period." I relayed the details back to her sharply.

"Yes, that's correct. Oh and remember, chemistry, it is important to build a good rapport. Chemistry will separate you from the rest. Any problems call Dino, safety first. Good luck Rose."

"Thank you," I replied, filled with anxiety.

Something about what Isabella said made me feel like she really cared about me. I knew she probably said that to all the girls but it was the way she said my name it was so endearing. She spoke my name with so much care, even if it was an alias, it still felt good to hear. My mama always said my name with so much love. I missed my mama badly, that's probably what had me going soft. I pushed the sentiment aside I needed to focus on the matter at hand.

My hair, nails and feet all had to be done before the date. Back in the day whenever I was going out I always made sure I had an appointment booked with my hairstylist and one at the nail salon. However, right now I couldn't afford the VIP treatment, until I got my money back up I would have to take care of them myself. Choosing something to wear was hard, half of my wardrobe was still at Cam's, think of Carrie's closet in the 'Sex and the City' movie but bigger.

I hated living out of a suitcase but was grateful for the little I had with me. I laid out a few dresses on the bed and managed to narrow it down to two. I was torn between my Julia Clancey baby-doll dress and my coral blush one shoulder draped dress by Donna Karan. Donna Karan won because it matched my Balenciaga giant envelope clutch and Salvatore Ferragamo tilapia sandals perfectly.

Outfit was sorted, now I had to try and work the same magic on my hair. I had already decided to keep it simple so just straighten it and curled my fringe under slightly to give it a nice bounce. I painted my nails and toes red and managed to get ready just before Dino called to tell me he was waiting downstairs.

We arrived at Nobu just before eight o' clock. My gosh I was so nervous, I could not believe that I was actually going ahead with this. What was I thinking? This was against everything I believed in. Assariyah Jones a fucking escort. An escort was just a fancy label for a prostitute. My daddy would be rolling over in his grave right now and if Mama ever found out this would surely send her to hers. There was no way I could subject myself to such lows.

"I can't do this, I can't go through with this," I said shaking my head.

"First time jitters...huh?" Dino asked.

"I can't go in there Dino, please take me back to my hotel."

"All the girls are exactly like you the first time but once you do your first client you'll be fine," he said, attempting to reassure me.

I still felt apprehensive about the whole situation.

"I'm not sure about this Dino. What if something happens to me?"

"C'mon Rose I'm here, I won't let anything bad happen to you. Trust me!"

"Promise."

"I promise," he repeated, sincerely.

I replenished my make-up before stepping out of the car.

"Rose," I turned back to face Dino at the sound of his call. "You look beautiful, first sign of trouble call me and remember you are one of the smart ones. You get paid to do what other girls give out for free."

His words boosted my confidence. I smiled, "Thanks D," and headed towards the door. Dino was so right I was getting paid to get laid while the other dumb bitches gave it out for free.

Upon arrival one of the reception staff took my reservation details and then led me to my table. To my relief, Tim Bakhtin was already there. I wouldn't have been able to stick it out sitting on my own waiting for him to show up. I took a seat and flashed him a smile, he reciprocated the gesture. I studied his features, he had blonde hair and striking grey eyes. He looked different to what I had expected but then again I guess I really didn't know what to expect. I was impressed by his dress sense, he was wearing one of Emporio Armani's tailored two button suits. Something about his demeanour reminded me of Richard Gere in 'Pretty Woman', so far so good.

The man from reception walked away and business commenced immediately.

"How are you Rose?" he asked, slipping me a brown envelope.

"I'm good thank you," I replied, whilst discretely putting the envelope under my clutch bag. I looked around the room and spotted a few celebrities. As the glitterati mingled I couldn't help wondering how many other couples exchanged envelopes that night. I was glad he handed over the money without me prompting him, Isabella had informed me that getting the cash out the way first was proper escort etiquette. I excused myself and headed to the bathroom. I counted three thousand and five hundred pounds in total. Wow, it felt good holding cash again!

I separated Isabella's twenty percent deduction and pocketed two thousand and eight hundred pounds. Money was precious to Isabella, she didn't take kindly to people who tried to pull a fast one on her. Dino had told me story about one of the girls who tried to be slick and steal money from Isabella. The girl ended up with acid thrown on her face, she was left disfigured and never worked again. The message was clear, Isabella was a powerful woman who had connections and she wasn't to be fucked with.

I headed back to the table to join Tim.

I whispered, "You want four hours."

"Yes," he nodded.

Shortly afterwards a waitress came over to take our order. I spotted the Bluefin Toro on the menu and, although it sounded delicious, I was not about to start eating endangered species so opted for the Black Cod. Tim went for the Yellowtail Sashimi with Jalapeno. He also ordered Saké and I drank cocktails. As we indulged in our meal, Tim told me about his background. He was born and raised in Russia where he had made his fortune in the iron and steel industry. He asked me about myself, I made up a persona and told him I was working to save up for med school. I know, crazy right, but it was the first thing that came out of my mouth. I figured that if he asked any questions I could always use some of the stories Jasmina had told me about her experiences in the med school world.

We had a good conversation over dinner. He made me laugh when he told me that I looked like Naomi Campbell and Beyonce. "Aaah you are so beautiful Rose, you look like that bootylicious singer and the model Naomi Campbell." I shook my head, laughing and asked myself why all European men act like Naomi and Beyonce are the only two black women in the world. It was all good though.

I was disappointed when dinner was over and Tim paid for the bill because I knew what time it was. Tim hailed down a black taxi outside Nobu and we headed back to his hotel. I texted Dino so that he would follow us to our destination. By the time we got back to the hotel there was an hour and a half left on the clock. Tim dimmed the lights and turned on some music. Lisa

Stansfield's voice filled the room, changing the atmosphere to one best suited for lovers. He grabbed me by the waist and leaned in for a kiss but I gave him my neck instead. I did not feel comfortable kissing him on the lips just yet. My neck was my hot spot and under usual circumstances my juices would have been flowing within minutes but this was far from usual for me.

Tim leaned in for a kiss again, my body tighten up.

"Relax, why are you so tense?" Tim asked, rubbing my shoulders.

I bit my bottom lip as I always did whenever I was nervous.

"I'm sorry, I don't know what's wrong with me tonight."

Tim reached in his pocket and handed me a blue pill with an imprinted smiley face. "Take this it will make you feel better."

"What is it?" I asked warily.

"Oooh this is nothing, it's harmless, it's only ecstasy," he said, throwing a blue pill in his mouth.

I had never taken drugs but I needed something to loosen up. I was shit scared and didn't think I could go all the way but he had already paid and the money was too appealing to give back, so I followed suit.

Thirty minutes later the 'E' began to kick in. I had an energy buzz and felt more alive and alert than I had felt before. Everything around me looked more vibrant. Tim looked better than I recalled and his touch felt more intense. He was rubbing against my breast and it was just so electrifying.

I didn't stop to think twice when he asked me to suck

his dick and dropped to my knees. Tim was my first experience with a pink dick and I wasn't sure if it was the 'E' playing tricks on me but, contrary to popular belief, his package was not tiny. It was not close to what I was used to but it was a healthy size.

I had mastered the art of oral down to perfection. I had his balls in one hand and his cock in the other. I wet my lips and placed my top lip over my teeth before putting his cock in my mouth. I worked my way up from his shaft to the top, gently squeezing his balls. His breathing intensified as he moaned with pleasure. I lubricated my fingers with oil and inserted my index finger into his asshole just like he instructed me to do. I felt his balls tightening up and knew he was about to cum so I took him out of my mouth and gently blew on his dick. Tim's body trembled as I continued working his asshole. He started fingering me and stuck his fingers in and out my pussy several times before licking off my juices. He then placed me at the edge of the bed and held my legs over his shoulders and fucked me for twenty minutes straight until we finally came together in unison.

Tim thanked me for a lovely evening and I gathered my things and left. Dino drove me back to my hotel. As soon as I got in I had a long shower and scrubbed my body raw. The effects of the ecstasy began to wear off and the guilt began to kick in. Did I really just put a price on my vay jay jay?

I picked up my diary, I hadn't touched it since the wedding but my emotions were running high. I didn't know who I was becoming and needed a release. Writing was just so therapeutic for my soul, I wasn't sure I even had one anymore but I wrote and wrote for hours until I dosed off.

I met with Isabella the following afternoon to give her share of the money. She smiled non-stop as she counted the cash.

"I love the way money feels in my hands."

"I know the feeling," I replied.

"How did you find the experience with ummm… Tim Bakhtin?"

"It was different to anything I have ever done before."

"Different how exactly…have you never had sex before?"

I laughed at Isabella's joke. She told me that Tim had told her that whenever he was next in town he only wanted her to send me. I admit that was quite flattering to hear.

With money in my hands again I went flat hunting. I had been searching for the last couple of days but didn't see anything that warmed to me until the estate agent showed me the E1 Waterside apartment. The reception room, high specification kitchen and two bedrooms with en-suite bathrooms were furnished to my taste. The floor to ceiling windows and the balcony gave me a beautiful view of the River Thames. With rent at just six hundred and twenty five pounds per week I could make the monthly rent money in one night. I loved it and told the estate agent that I'd take it. With the money I made the night before I left a deposit of one thousand five hundred pounds and paid the weekly rate in advance. I signed the leasing documents and the estate agent handed me the keys. As soon as I added a few signatures pieces like the Damson Taupe Milliner chair I wanted, I knew that I would have a place to call home.

CHAPTER 8

In the space of a few months I managed to build up a nice client base of wealthy, high profile men. I experienced men of all races, dicks of all shapes and sizes. At a point I was having sex three times a day, seven days a week. Isabella loved me I was so good for her business that her and Dino even nicknamed me their V.I.P (Very Insatiable Pussy) doll. I didn't know how to stop once the money came rolling in. I wasn't sure I even wanted to.

Some people worked in offices staring at a computer screen all day, others stacked shelves, doctors saved lives, some mothers choose to stay at home to look after their babies. I chose to satisfy the needs and desires of grown ass men. It was just another occupation to me. I learned to detach any feelings of love from sex, once I removed that attachment the job became easier and I didn't need to rely on 'E' pills to feel good.

I enjoyed the perks that came with the job, especially travelling. I saw some of the most beautiful places in the world, Dubai, Thailand, Paris, Greece, Milan, New York, Bahamas, Seychelles, St Tropez, Las Vegas and St Barts to name a few. I dined at exclusive restaurants; The Ivy, The Ritz, Zuma, Hakkasan, Mr Chow etc, you name it, chances are I'd probably been there. I attended various events, ranging from fashion shows to football games to boring corporate parties. I rekindled my love for the arts with regular visits to the theatre, opera, ballet and museums. Cameron had always been too busy working to take me so I eventually stopped going.

I have had far too many encounters to recall. I stopped counting when I hit the five hundred mark. I can't tell you about every single one of my experiences but I will share some of the ones that had the most significant impact on my life. I really don't know where to start but here it goes. I only ever accepted outcall jobs, the rates were much higher. Plus there was no way in hell that I was gonna let these motherfuckers find out where I laid my head on the rare occasion that I actually got to sleep in my own bed. Judge me if you want but there is nothing you can say or think that I haven't already thought or called myself.

Paul Davies, or Dennis, to be honest I can't remember his surname but it was one of the two. I was crazy excited about that job because of the money. It was an overnight call which meant that I would pocket ten grand...yep ten grand! I met Paul at Vertigo 42 as planned. After the usual formalities of collecting the brown envelope and counting the cash was out the way we sat back to sip champagne against the London skyline and enjoyed the amazing view. After our third bottle my head was filled with bubbles, I wasn't drunk just tipsy, we headed back to Paul's place in Belgravia. When we got there a busty high yellow chick opened the door. I automatically assumed that she was his live in house help or something and thought nothing of her. Well that was until she grabbed his face and started tonguing the shit out of him.

"I've been waiting, what took you so long darling?" she asked him when she finally came up for air.

"Okay, what the fuck is going on here?" I asked, astounded.

"Oh I'm sorry Rose, this is my wife Tia."

"Your wife," I managed to blurt out. "What exactly is this?"

"Paul did you not tell her the plan?" his wife asked.

"Look I don't know what is going on here but Isabella didn't mention anything about a third party. I'm afraid I don't get down like that, I'll give you half of your money back but I'm outta here."

"Paul do something," I heard Tia say as I threw half of the money he had given me earlier on the floor.

I left them standing in the hallway and walked out on them closing the door firmly behind me. I ran down the stairs, praying that I wouldn't break my neck in my six inch heels.

"Wait, please hold on," Paul hollered out of breath as he caught up with me. "Please don't go."

"Give me one good reason why I should stay, Isabella didn't tell me anything about this ménage trios shit."

"That's because she doesn't know, I didn't tell her. You see my wife has had this crazy fantasy for years about sleeping with another woman, it's our wedding anniversary tomorrow and we couldn't think of a better way of seeing it through."

"Okay happy anniversary and all but y'all are gonna have to find another girl."

"No, no, no you don't understand we have been searching for weeks, looked at thousand of girls but Tia you know, she wasn't satisfied until she saw your profile."

"I'm honoured, honestly I am but I can't go there."

"If you stay I'll give you an extra ten thousand."

My eyes lit up, my palms were itching but there were some things that even I couldn't do. I wasn't down with the whole carpet munching shit. What Kinda person did I look like?

"I'm sorry Paul, I just can't do it."

I didn't get very far up Belgravia Square before I decided to do a complete u-turn. I couldn't say no to that sort of money and if I went through with it I would get back the money I threw on the floor before walking out. Money over everything I reminded myself before plucking up the courage to knock on their door. Paul opened the door, the huge smile across his face made me realise how important this was to them.

"Thank you," Paul mouthed.

"Ten grand extra, right?"

He nodded, I'll get it for you now and add it to the money that you left behind."

That was music to my ears. Isabella knew nothing about the extra ten grand so she couldn't tax that. All I had to give her was two thousand and I would pocket eighteen grand. Geez I can't believe I almost walked away from money. Thank God almost doesn't count.

"I'm so glad you came back, what can I get you to drink?" Tia asked.

"Nothing I'm good thanks."

"You sure?"

"Yeah I'm sure," I replied, just wanting the night to be over and done with already.

She smiled at me seductively releasing her long red locks from the ponytail it was held up in. Tia undressed herself and knelt right before me. She leaned in and caressed my face. I didn't know how to react, I was strictly dickly, this was a brand new territory for me but they were paying so I had to oblige.

"Beauty of a rose, so immaculate," she marvelled as she ran her fingers across my lips. It was just too weird for me, being around her made me feel nervous. She pressed her lips against mine and sucked on my lips. Her heart shaped lips were soft and cushion like. She tasted like strawberries and smelt of Trish McEvoy Snowdrop and Crystal Flowers, one of my favourite fragrances. She had style, I could tell from the pristine decor in their home. I tried to distract my mind from the situation at hand by focusing on everything but Tia but that failed. Every time she touched me I felt shivers running through my body. The woman knew what she was doing, no ifs, no buts about that.

The next thing I knew she had me completely naked and was sucking on my nipples with varied intensity. No man had ever responded to my body the way Tia did, I'm not saying she was better but the feeling was different. I can't really explain it but it was like she was in my brain and knew exactly where to touch, where to lick and just how much pressure and intensity to apply at the precise moment my body needed her to. She pushed my thighs apart placing them on either side of the chair and used her tongue to trace the outline of my pussy. Within seconds I was soaking wet. She was licking and sucking, biting and pulling, fingering me and rubbing on my clit. She brought out a different side of me.

The reserved girl that entered the room had been replaced by an untamed feline in the wild. She had me moaning like crazy, my eyes rolled to the back of my head. I held on to the arms of the chair for dear life as she continued to tongue my pussy to death.

When Tia finally came up for air she stood in front of me and guided my fingers to her hot spot. I inserted two fingers into Tia's wet pussy, she let out a soft moan.

"Ummmm that feels sooooo good, don't stop."

At that point Paul walked into the room, butt naked, holding his dick in his hand. He had been watching us. I had seen him looking through the crack in the door, he was bashing himself off which turned me on even more.

"You girls are putting on quite a show."

Tia glanced over to her husband and signalled for him to come over. Without delay Paul placed Tia on all fours and rammed his cock into her pussy. The way she moaned made me feel jealous, I needed some cock in me too.

As I watched Paul fuck Tia I inserted my fingers in and out of my pussy vigorously. I wasn't sure if she would let her husband fuck me but I needed him to. I licked Paul's balls as he pumped himself in and out of Tia and to my delight he responded. He laid me down and fucked me missionary style on the floor. Tia not wanting to be left out the action sat on my face and I sucked on her pussy. Our moans filled the room as we continued to fuck each other. Our bodies shook uncontrollably, we had our own mini earthquake as we came one after the other.

I let Tia and Paul use me anyway they pleased and when my time was up I collected my belongings and wished them happy anniversary before I left.

Tia replied grinning, "Oh it's not our anniversary but when it is we will definitely include you in our celebrations."

They had tricked me but they had also treated me in more ways than I had bargained for, everything was even.

CHAPTER 9

Do you know what it feels like to be owned? Well if you don't already know, I pray that you never have to find out. I can only describe it as the most degrading feeling in the world. Imagine someone controlling your actions and emotions. Telling you how to feel and what to do, whenever they felt like it. In the end you only have yourself to blame because you allowed them to put a price on you.

You may have realised that I have only mentioned the perks of the job and the good times that I had but, as you know, everything in life has its good and its bad. I had been lucky that most of my clients were good people just looking for a great time but it only takes one person or moment to fuck it all up.

This next incident is really difficult for me to talk about but I feel like I need to tell you this. I won't go into every detail because the memory is one that I prefer to keep etched in my subconscious.

It was just like any other booking. Isabella gave me

the details and I showed up ready for whatever. With John Mews, like many other jobs I had done before there was no prelude to the show, it was straight fucking and I was cool with that. Sometimes I couldn't stand the pretence or the small talk, racking my brain endlessly trying to come up with ideas for a stimulating conversation with a brainless mutt. At times it was really better to skip the talking and stick to fucking.

Unlike my other jobs where I was treated to the best of everything, John chose a rundown hostel for our meeting spot. When Dino first dropped me off, I asked him to double check that it was the right place and was horrified to find out that it was indeed. I was sceptical about going in because I had this stereotype in my head of hostels being filled with junkies running up and down with needles hanging out their arms. To my relief there was no sign of madness in the hallway as I headed to room number forty-five, but the closer I got to the room the more unsettled I felt. I never should have entered that room but I pushed all the eerie feelings I had aside, telling myself to chill and quit acting like a boujis bitch.

The door was slightly ajar so I just walked in.

"Take off your clothes."

Those were his exact words to me, not even a hello. I laughed.

"Wow, you move fast," I said, trying to ease the tension in the room.

"Take off your clothes," he repeated again.

"Okay I get it you wanna get straight to business but nothing is going to happen unless I see some money first."

"You'll get your money later," he scowled.

What a douche bag I thought. It was common knowledge that escorts did not perform until payment was sorted.

"No money, no action," I said, teasingly, still trying to lighten the mood but his facial expression remained unchanged.

He walked over to a little stand across the room and grabbed a wad of cash and waved it at me.

"I've got money, now take off your clothes," he said as he handed over the cash.

I took off my clothes and stood in the middle of the room completely naked. Even though I had been naked in front of men numerous of times, the way he glared at me made me feel very uncomfortable.

"You black whore bitch, don't just stand there, put them on," he said, pointing to the skin tight leather outfit with a matching face mask on the bed. The bed looked like it had been infested with a million and one cum stains and someone forgot to change the sheets. I spotted the whip on the floor. Now I was cool with role play but this shit was just way too much. He was taking this to a whole other level but, as they say, different strokes for different folks. I knew one thing for sure though, if there was any whipping taking place I'd be the one lashing out. My skin was way too smooth and beautiful to pick up scars over one dude's freaky fetish. The quicker I got this over with the sooner I could get outta there.

"Arrrrrgggghhhh," I screamed out in pain from the bastard pulling me down to the floor by my hair. "What are you playing at? I'm leaving."

"You're not going anywhere, I've paid for you now

I'm going to treat you like the tramp you are."

His eyes were filled with so much fury and that really frightened the hell out of me. My heart was racing, something wasn't right about this guy and I wanted out. I ran towards the door but he got there before me and blocked the exit.

"Move out my way," I ordered.

"Or what, bitch?" he growled, slapping me across my face.

I cried out in pain, rubbing the side of my cheek.

"Just let me go please."

"Be careful what you wish for whore." He pulled a knife out of his pocket then pushed me down on the bed pressing the knife against my throat. "I'll let you go to your maker but first I'm going to have fun with you."

He unzipped his trousers and smirked at me as he slapped his dick across my face. Tears filled my eyes and started streaming down my face. I did not want to die, especially not like this, but the more I tried to fight him the more pain he inflicted on me. I tried to scream but he shoved his dick in my mouth to silence me. I bit down hard on his penis and watched him grimace in pain. This made him extra mad, he ran his blade all over me threatening to slash my face. He continued to slap me and choke me with his dick, making me suck him off against my will.

I needed this to be over, I couldn't stomach this bastard being inside me, with every pump and thrust I wanted the ground to open up and swallow me. He closed his eyes but never stopped yelling profanities at me. His eyes were closed but I knew that he could open them any minute so I had to be super quick. I reached into my bag which was on the floor and felt around for my phone and speed dialled Dino's number. I prayed that he would be able sense that something was wrong. I never called him on a job but I needed him now.

"Please let me go," I cried out loudly, hoping that Dino could hear me.

"Don't worry as soon as I cum, I'm gonna slash you into pieces filthy whore."

The torture did not stop. He was biting me, pulling and ramming his dick forcefully in and out my hole. Every time I thought he was coming the pain just intensified. It had been ten minutes or so since I called Dino but there was still no sign of him. I had given up hope that he would find me in time. I prayed silently in my head trying to block out thoughts of John shouting, "I'm gonna take pleasure in slashing you all over before giving you a golden shower."

"You don't have to do this," I said, trying to reason with him.

He simply laughed at me and grabbed his whip, he was just about to hit me but the knock on the door distracted his attention.

"Rose, Rose, are you in there Rose?" I heard Dino calling out frantically.

"Dino help…" I started to scream but before I could finish, John began strangling me, cutting off my air supply.

"Shut up or I'll kill both you and your friend."

"Open the door now," Dino yelled, not giving John a chance to answer he broke down the door instantly. Rushing in he grabbed John off me and punched him in the face, John punched him back. The two men began to scuffle until Dino finally overpowered John. Dino kicked John in his balls causing him to fall to the ground in excruciating pain, "You sick fuck, I'm gonna make sure you never forget this day. Come here Rose, imprint your initials on this punk's forehead," he handed me John's knife.

I was trembling all over, I wanted to hurt him so badly but couldn't. Shaking my head I told Dino that I couldn't do it. He was furious, "You can't let him get away with this shit Rose."

Dino took the knife off me and carved my initials 'RM' into the middle of John's forehead. It was a sickening sight, blood was gushing out of his skin and he screamed out in agony.

"Rose Monet, don't you ever forget that sick bastard," I spat on his face before walking out.

Dino carried me out through the back door of the hostel. "I'm so sorry Rose, I promised to never let anything happen to you and I let you down."

"It's not your fault D, thank you for coming through when you did." He tried to convince me to go to the hospital but I insisted that I was okay, I just needed to rest. Dino stayed with me that night, I didn't want to be alone.

I woke up around noon the next day. My body still ached tremendously and I couldn't get the images out of my head. I was so jumpy, every sound I heard made me panic. I forgot that Dino had stayed the night and screamed when I heard movements in my kitchen.

"Relax Rose, it's only me," Dino said, as he brought

me breakfast in bed. I couldn't eat it and pushed it aside.

"How are you feeling?" Dino asked.

Without saying a word I rested my head on his shoulders, I needed to feel safe.

"Rose I want you to have this. I bought it for you this morning. Make sure you carry it with you on every job."

I looked down at the Snub-nose .38 special Dino held out for me and told him I couldn't take it. I no longer felt safe, I had to leave Precision Escorts. What if I wasn't so lucky next time? I couldn't deal with this shit anymore.

"Precision won't be the same without you Rose, but I respect your wishes."

I smiled and gave him a tight hug, "Thanks D."

"Look, Rose I want you to have this it will make me sleep better."

I took the pistol from Dino and hugged him again. He kissed me on my forehead. "Stay beautiful and don't you ever think twice about pulling that trigger."

I closed the door behind Dino and fell to the ground weeping. If only I felt as beautiful on the inside as everyone kept telling me that I looked on the outside. That's the thing about life though, everything is never what it really appears to be but, by the time most people realise this, it is already too late. I was in deep and I knew that I would have to dig deeply to find myself once again. Enough was enough. I would not continue to dance to the beat of someone else's drum.

CHAPTER 10

I had made up my mind that I would not do the whole escort thing again. I already said my goodbyes to Dino and Isabella so the last person I expected to show up on my caller I.D was Isabella. At first when the phone rang I was sure she had dialled my number in error so I left the phone to ring out but then she called for the second, third and fourth time. In the end I picked up to find out what she wanted. I prayed that nothing bad had happened to Dino. John was a psycho, what if he had gone after Dino? All sorts of crazy thoughts were running through my mind.

"Hey Isabella, is everything okay?"

"Aah yes everything is fine darling. How are you holding up?" She didn't give me a chance to answer, "I'm sorry about what happened to you Rose but business just isn't the same without you. Won't you please consider coming back?"

I was shocked by what I was hearing, "I can't believe you would even ask me that Isabella. In case you've forgotten I nearly died on the last job I did for you." I was so offended.

"Rose I really wouldn't ask this of you if it wasn't important. I'm asking you for one last favour please."

"No way Isabella, I'm staying out the game."

She pleaded, "At least listen to the details first."

I knew it had to be pretty serious because Isabella wasn't the type to beg for anything.

"Two weeks in Miami, all expenses paid, plus seventy grand for each week you are out there."

"I'm not interested, you're gonna have to send one of the other girls."

"Don't you think I've already tried that? The client will not hear of it, he wants you. He saw your profile online a couple of weeks before we took it down and he called to enquire about you. Do this last job my V.I.P doll and you'll have over one hundred grand behind you. Think about it," she said and put the phone down promptly.

I listened to the sound of the rain falling against my window pane and reflected on my life. A week had gone by since my last conversation with Isabella. Ever since then I had been in a state of hibernation. I'd stayed in bed watching the minutes run into hours and the hours turning into days. My life was one big mess. I had no friends, no husband or children and had not spoken to my family in months. In hindsight I really had nothing to lose if I took the job. I wanted to cry but couldn't, I was all out of tears.

Isabella's proposal weighed heavily on my mind but I still couldn't come to a decision. I decided to leave it in the hands of fate and tossed a coin in the air. Heads for Miami, tails for London. Fate had decided, I dragged myself out of bed and went shopping. It was wet outside but popping tags always made me feel better so it was a small price to pay.

I stacked up on several luxury pieces but my favourite purchase was a camouflage Rose gown by Alexander McQueen, it was beyond fabulous. The man had been a creative genius. I really couldn't imagine the fashion world without him now that he was gone. I grabbed my Louis luggage and dumped my new items into them. I was rubbish at packing, more times than not I packed way too much stuff. The travelling light gene definitely skipped me but someone had to show those Americans how we Europeans got down when it came to Fashion.

I had a preliminary meeting with Stephen Richards in the Garden Room at Lanesborough Hotel later on that evening. When I walked in, he spotted me and signalled for me to come over to his table. At a first glance, he left me feeling breathless. He was so handsome, I'm talking about Morris Chestnut eat your heart out type of handsome. Next to Tyler he was probably the second hottest guy I had ever seen in my life.

"Good evening beautiful, what can I get you to drink?" Stephen asked, as he lit a Cuban cigar. Not wanting anything too strong, I ordered a Malibu and pineapple. I sat inhaling the smoke from Stephen's cigar and wondered why I always got stuck with the smokers. This was probably Shelia's idea of a joke from up above. It was always a bitter sweet moment whenever I smelt or saw someone light a cigarette in my presence, I couldn't help but think of her. I imagined what she thought of me at that moment. A sense of shame fell over me, I promised myself this was my last job, hoping that she could read my thoughts wherever she was.

Once my drink arrived, Stephen handed me a briefcase full of money. "I apologise that this is a very brief meeting but I trust that you have all the details you need."

I nodded my head, I didn't have time to count the money but from the weight of the case alone I knew it was sound.

"Good, as you know I'm flying out tomorrow night so I'll be there waiting for you. See you in a couple of days."

I wished him a safe journey and left.

On my way back home I held on to the briefcase for dear life. I hailed down a black cab which literally dropped me outside my house but that didn't stop me from looking over my shoulders every five seconds. Carrying all that money had me on edge. When I finally got home I was super relieved. I immediately emptied the contents of the briefcase unto my bed. Brand-new crisp fresh fifty-pound notes scattered all over my bed, Sir John Houblon never looked so good! I grabbed a stack and sniffed it. I loved the smell of money, it made me so excited and I couldn't stop myself from screaming as I tossed it in the air.

Money over everything I repeated to myself as I counted the money over and over again. Stephen had paid half of the money straight away, the second half would be paid when the job was completed. I counted seventy-three thousand pounds in total. The extra three grand was for me to book my flight. I counted the money one last time and took out Isabella's deduction, minus fourteen-thousand pounds. Damn it hurt! That was always the most painful part for me, giving her money for my hard work, but it had to be done.

I flipped open my MacBook Pro and searched for flights from London Heathrow to Miami International. I preferred booking my own flights, it was less hassle that way and prevented clients from finding out that my name wasn't really Rose Monet but Assariyah Jones. The less they knew about me the better, especially now that I was leaving the game for good.

CHAPTER 11

I looked at my alarm clock, it read 08:30am. It took a while for my brain to register the time but when it did, I immediately went into panic mode and jumped out of bed. Shit! I had a flight to catch, how could I have overslept? I woke up an hour later than I had planned which threw me completely off balance. I ran around like a headless chicken trying to get all my shit together. I literally just popped out the shower when the chauffeur from Virgin Atlantic arrived to take me to the airport. Ground transfers were part of the perks of upper class bookings.

Luckily I had laid out my airport outfit the night before. I threw on a pair of black skin-tight jeans and a black T-shirt cut out in the shape of a butterfly. I had no time to do my make-up and grabbed my all black Gucci shades from the breakfast table as I was heading out. They were a life saver, they disguised all beauty sins that came in the form of dark circles and bags as a result of sleep deprivation on my part.

The driver put my bags in the car. "Miss Jones, hope you've got everything, passport, tickets, money," he said just before pulling off.

Yawning, I replied, "I'm sure I have." I was about to lay back and sleep when something told me to look in my bag for safe measure.

"Shit! Oh my gosh turn around," I instructed the driver. "My passport isn't in my bag."

"You'll need to be quick, if you don't want to miss your flight. We are running slightly off schedule."

I hated when people stated the obvious. I replied slightly irritated, "Well there is no point in being on schedule without my passport."

I ran as fast as the Louboutin open toe booties I was wearing would let me. The front door was double locked, taking double the time to open it. Time was against me and everything just seemed to take double long. I glanced at my watch, it was 09:30am, the flight was due to depart at 11:15am. Fuck! I had to be super quick. I searched my bedroom frantically, practically turning it upside down but it wasn't there. I created the same mess in the living room but I didn't find it there either. The driver was tooting his horn downstairs which wasn't helping my nerves. I took a deep breath and decided to retrace my steps again.

U-N-F-U-C-K-I-N-G B-E-L-I-E-V-A-B-L-E! The shit was on my breakfast table. It had been staring at me all along. Trust me to remember my shades but leave my passport behind. I was so back to front some times. I couldn't help laughing at myself and hurried back downstairs.

"Got it," I said, waving my passport at the driver.

"I'm not sure we will make it on time," he replied.

I pleaded, "Please try and drive as fast as you can," and sat back praying for the best.

We didn't arrive at the airport until 10:30am. I wasn't sure I'd make it but I had to try. We rushed through Terminal 3 at Heathrow and headed to Virgin's check-in point. I managed to check my bags in fairly quickly, because I was travelling first class, I didn't have to queue for hours in line to check in. I thanked the driver for his help and made my way through to security.

The announcements showed that my flight VS005 had already started boarding. I heard my name being called for the flight and ran towards the gate after being cleared by security. I was the last to board so the whole plane was staring at me because I had kept them waiting. I was slightly embarrassed but was more happy that I actually caught my flight. I sat back and wiped the beads of sweat from my forehead. In about nine hours or so I would be in Miami.

We landed around 4pm local time, I was pleased to see that my luggage had also arrived safely. I had too many valuable goods in them and couldn't afford for anything to go missing. I grabbed a trolley for convenience and was about to call a taxi when I spotted a chauffeur holding a card with my name on it. I totally forgot that ground transfers applied on the other end of the trip too.

I walked up to him and greeted him, "Hello, I'm Assariyah Jones."

He shook my hand and smiled. "Good afternoon

Miss Jones. How was your flight?"

"We had a little turbulence but other than that there is not much to complain about when you're in first class."

We both laughed and proceeded to the car. I confirmed that I was staying at the Setai hotel on Collins Avenue, which was situated right in the heart of South Beach. I looked out the window, admiring the beautiful palm trees lined up on the streets as the driver and I engaged in small talk. I was already in love with the place. The sun was shining, with the temperature at 32°c, Miami was a tropical paradise and I was so glad to be away from freezing London.

Thirty minutes later and I was at the Setai. I immediately fell in love with the hotel, it was ultra stylish, just way too beautiful for words. I gave the hotel's receptionist my details and she told me that they were expecting me.

"Oh yes, Mr Richards told us that you would be arriving today Ms Monet. You'll be staying in the Imperial Suite. The concierge will help you up to the penthouse. Hope you enjoy your stay with us."

I smiled and thanked her.

The concierge carried my luggage up. I gave him fifty dollars to show my appreciation. Americans were big on tips and frowned upon non-tippers so I always tipped big. Stephen was not there when I arrived but he had left a message to inform me that he had a meeting to attend but he would be back in the evening. I took the opportunity to explore the penthouse and the more I saw of it, the more I knew that it would be hard for me to leave. It was a place where I wanted to live forever. We had an oceanfront view, it was heaven. 'Palace in the sky' was the perfect description for the Imperial Suite, it was beyond magnificent. Everything from the exclusive roof terrace equipped with a pool and garden, down to the black granite flooring was immaculate. As they say in Spanish, esto es lo que yo llamo la buena vida! (This is what I call the good life!)

The penthouse cost about thirty thousand dollars per night and we had it booked for fourteen days, I mean you do the math. Stephen was balling big time! I made a mental note to ask him what type of business he was into because I wanted in. I needed a new way of keeping my money up. I wanted out of the escort business but didn't want to see my money slipping. Not having any money was not right, it was a no go, a major failure. It was time for me to start thinking differently. After the holiday I needed to plan my next move carefully, that I knew for sure.

I was starving so I ordered room service. Stephen was still not back yet and I had been there for five hours by myself. My eyes were beginning to feel heavy, the effects of the long flight were taking its toll on me but I fought off the sleep. I wanted to be awake when Stephen got back, so I stripped down and sat out in the pool to keep myself occupied. The oceanfront view was stunning. I loved the smell of the ocean and combined with the sound of the waves it was absolutely tranquil. I closed my eyes and dreamed of what life could have been like with Cameron if that bitch Jasmina had just kept her big mouth shut.

When I opened my eyes I was shocked to see Stephen standing over me. "Oh my gosh, how long have you been standing there for?" I asked, using my hands to cover up my bare breasts. He just laughed.

"You don't have to cover up, I was enjoying the view."

I was so embarrassed. I was about to jump out of the pool and reached for the towel by the edge of the pool when Stephen placed his hands over mine to stop me. "Don't end the party before it has even started Rose," he said, taking off his suit and joining me in the pool. Stephen was so damn sexy, the sight of his naked body next to me had my temperature rising. He grabbed my hips, pulling me closer to him, he placed gentle kisses over my lips, my neck and my collar bone before moving down to my breasts. He eliminated all elements of sleepiness from my body. I was wide awake and ready to receive his loving.

Stephen whispered into my ears, "Tell me exactly what you want me to do to you."

"Fuck me real hard baby, make me cum."

He smiled and pushed my legs apart then lifted me up slightly, giving him easier access to my prized jewel. I gasped, allowing a soft moan to escape my lips as he thrust his cock deep inside me.

He groaned with pleasure as he pushed his hardness in and out of me.

"Aaaah your pussy feels so good Rose."

He started off slowly but quickly increased his speed, the faster he moved the deeper his thrusts were. I loved the way he felt inside me and clenched my pussy muscles against his dick to maximise the pleasure. I rocked my hips to his rhythm, matching him thrust for thrust. I felt Stephen's body tighten up.

I dug my nails deep into his back and wailed in ecstasy, "Ooohh ahhhh I'm comingggggggg," as he shot a full load of cum into my hot pussy.

Stephen slapped my ass and told me to get ready. "The night life here is crazy! You'll love it," he said and helped me out the pool. I had a quick shower and decided to wear one of my Proenza Schouler dresses. I stood in front of the mirror adding a few finishing touches.

"You look beautiful," Stephen said, pleased with the effort I had made.

"Thank you, you don't look half bad yourself." I was ready to see what Miami had to offer.

It did not take long for us to reach our destination. It was literally only about twenty streets away from us. We ended up at the LIV nightclub at the Fontainebleau beach hotel. We stepped out the car and Stephen threw his keys to the Valet.

"Look after my baby man," he said, referring to his Lambo. He tipped him and we headed into the club.

Stephen and I had our own private party in one of the skyboxes overlooking the main dance floor. The club had a good vibe, the music was pumping and people were bumping and grinding hard to the beats. I often caught them looking up in our direction, they probably wished that they were in our position but I envied them. I would have loved to have had the freedom that they had. You know dancing freely on the dance floor, having a ball of a time. The thing is after a while the novelty of VIP inside a club wears off. There is only so much champagne one can pop and then what? I was at that stage in my life too, the 'what next' stage. I had so many questions with no answers and to say I was confused would have been an understatement.

For the next couple of weeks it was basically the same thing. Stephen went to handle his business early in the morning and didn't return till late in the evening, so the only time we really spent together was in the night. I wanted to occupy my days by sightseeing, taking a boat tour of Star Island, swimming with the dolphins, checking out the endangered species at Everglades. I wanted the opportunity to simply chill and laze out on South Beach soaking up the sun but Stephen was adamant that I stayed in the penthouse and didn't leave without him. My days were lonely but he had paid for my services and I had to oblige. I wasn't there to have my own fun. I was there for show, the perfect eye candy for him to show off and prance around town with like a trophy.

We would hit the clubs, come back to the penthouse and have sex. One evening I attended a charity event at the Versace Mansion with Stephen and I won a brand new digital camcorder from the raffle tickets I purchased. Soon after, Stephen was eager for us to return to the hotel so we could put the camera in motion. I on the other hand was not so thrilled about being filmed in action. The idea didn't sit right with me but Stephen promised that it was my camera and I could delete it if I did not like what I saw so I agreed.

Afterwards he played the recording back to me and I have to admit that seeing myself being fucked on camera turned me on a great deal. I felt so energised and geared up after watching it that we ended up fucking for five hours straight afterwards.

Looking back I don't know how Stephen did it, he hardly ever slept for more than a couple of hours each night but he was always full of energy. This might sound peculiar but when Stephen and I slept together at night, it was nice. Even though we were not actually a real couple, having the same person holding me night after night felt good, even if it was all make believe. Being with him made me realise what I was missing. I had been lonely for too long and a part of me was hoping that the holiday would never come to an end. Going home meant more loneliness. Although Stephen was only really available at night, at least he had been there and that was something. Back home there was nothing or nobody but me, myself, and I, and I wasn't in a rush to get back.

CHAPTER 12

When we got back to London, Stephen paid out the other seventy grand as promised. I paid Isabella her twenty percent and kept the remaining fifty six thousand. I had made a whopping one hundred and twelve thousand in total but was still unhappy. From the moment I got back from Miami I was not the same, my period was two weeks late and everything about me felt different. Overwhelmed with a huge sense of nostalgia, I missed the place so badly. I wanted to relive those magical moments of waking up to the serene view of the ocean every morning. In a weird kind of way, I also missed Stephen. I think I was in love with the idea of someone loving me enough to hold me tight at night and never letting go.

Three weeks after the trip I found myself comfort eating and ate and ate and ate, like there was no tomorrow. My waistline and derriere began expanding but I didn't really take much notice of the weight gain, until the day I tried on a pair of jeans and I couldn't do up the button. I convinced myself that they probably shrunk in the wash and grabbed another pair. Much to my dismay, the second pair was even tighter than the first ones I tried on. That was the wake-up call I needed and I immediately decided to sign up for Pilates again. However things did not go as planned. About twenty minutes back into my first Pilates class, I felt the room spinning, the instructor's voice became muffled and, before I knew it, my body gave way.

When I woke up I was in hospital, I had drips and all sorts of tubes attached to me. The nurse told me that she needed to take more blood from me and that they were still carrying out checks to identify what brought on the syncope.

"Syncope", I repeated. "What is that?"

"Oh I'm sorry Miss Jones. I didn't mean to scare you. Syncope is the medical term for fainting. One of the doctors will be along to see you shortly once we have all the results."

I despised hospitals and laying in one with the possibility of something being seriously wrong with me left me feeling scared and helpless. It also reinforced the fact that I could not carry on living without any contact with my family. Praying that I would be okay, I promised myself that, as soon as I was discharged, I would go and see my mum. It had been way too long, I hadn't seen her since my failed wedding to Cameron, the shame had been too much to bear.

Several hours later one of the doctors came to see me.

"How are you holding up Miss Jones?"

"I'm feeling a little tired but I'm okay I guess."

He smiled at me trying to put my mind at ease, "That is to be expected, you will find that you may suffer from fatigue a little more often now. You are pregnant Miss Jones."

"Pregnant, that's not possible."

He laughed, "It is six weeks possible. Once your temperature goes down, your release papers will be signed and you are free to go."

I still doubted what I was hearing, "Are you sure doctor?"

He nodded, "You are one hundred percent pregnant. The results will be referred to your GP. I suggest you book an appointment with him straight away. I have to go now but I'll try to see you before you leave."

I could not believe that I was pregnant. I was told that I would never be able to have a baby, so to actually be pregnant was somewhat a miracle. I remembered one of the girls at Precision telling me that 'some people get blessed doing the wrong things'. At the time I found it hard to fathom what she was saying but this was the perfect example. After all the madness I had been through, I was being blessed with the most precious gift in the world. For the first time in what felt like forever, I was absolutely happy but my joy soon turned bitter sweet.

Upon leaving the hospital I felt too drained to walk down five flights of stairs, so naturally I decided to wait for the lift. When the doors to the lift opened, I was frozen in a state of shock. It was like seeing a ghost, at first I thought my eyes were playing tricks on me, but that was not the case, she was real. It was definitely her, the very same bitch who destroyed my life was now trying to save lives.

Jasmina was standing right in front of me. My whole body was burning up, I was filled with rage. She evoked so much hate in me, my initial reaction was to lash out and throttle the shit out of her but my legs would not move. The doors slid shut and, just like that, she was gone. What hurt the most was the fact that I did not do anything about it. I could not risk harming the baby so I just let her walk away again.

CHAPTER 13

A couple of days went by before I decided to call Stephen and tell him the news. I had no idea about how he would react but he was the father and he had the right to know.

"Hey Stephen, it is Rose," I said, nervously.

"Hi Rose, how are you doing?"

I couldn't keep it in so I blurted out, "I'm pregnant with your baby."

He paused for a while then replied, "You don't seriously expect me to believe that it is mine?"

"Look, I understand why you have your doubts but you are the only person I have been with within the past six weeks."

"Well forgive me, forgive me for not taking the word of the town whore as gospel. Even if it is mine, and that is a very big IF, I want nothing to do with it."

"You bloody bastard, how dare you? That 'it' you are referring to is my baby and whether you like it or not, I'm going to have this baby."

"This will ruin everything, you cannot have it," he yelled.

I slammed the phone down and paced back and forth on my balcony in an attempt to calm myself down. Stress was the last thing I needed, especially at such an early stage into my pregnancy. I was going to do this shit and nobody was going to stop me from having my little miracle.

The conversation with him had taken me back to a place I did not ever want to remember. You see when I was fourteen I had fallen pregnant by Eric, my sister Nayla's boyfriend. He was twenty-two at the time and she was twenty. They had been dating for about three years so he was a regular fixture in our household. One day I had bumped into him after leaving school early. He'd asked what I was doing bunking off, so I told him I usually skipped Miss Preston's History class on Wednesday afternoons because Judy and her big mouth friends always hated on me. They would call me names and throw things at me but dumb ass Miss Preston was blind to all the shit they did. However the moment I retaliated and tried to stick up for myself, she all of a sudden got X-ray vision.

"Assariyah Jones why must you always find the need to disrupt my class? I'll tell you what, since you think you are so clever, come here and teach the class."

"But Miss they…"

"That is it get out of my class, you are on detention for a whole week."

The whole class erupted with laughter as I got up to leave the classroom. I hated them all and couldn't be bothered to keep getting in trouble just for defending myself, so I stopped going to her class altogether.

"I'll tell you what, come back to my place and you can chill out and play with my Nintendo, that way you don't have to worry about bumping into anyone else."

"For real? Thanks Eric," I said, giving him a big hug.

"No sweat baby girl but you've got to promise not to tell your sister or I'll be the one who is in big trouble."

"I promise, cross my heart and hope to die, promise."

He winked at me and I followed him to his place.

When we arrived at his house, Eric and I played computer games and he gave me loads of candy and chocolates. I was having so much fun until Eric started stroking my thighs.

I moved his hands away, "Eric what are you doing?"

"Lighten up Assariyah, I just wanna play a little game with you."

"I should really start going home now."

"We both know that if you go home now, you'll get in trouble for bunking off school."

I shrugged my shoulders even though he was right. It was way too early to go home, Mama would flip out.

"Just chill out," Eric said and then started kissing me. I knew what we were doing was totally wrong but it started to feel kind of good after a while and I did not have the strength or the will power to fight him so I laid still and let him have his way with me.

Fast forward three months and I found out that I was pregnant. When I told Eric, he told me that I had to get rid of it.

"I love your sister, if you have this baby it will ruin everything. She will hate you and your whole family will think you are a whore, do you see why you can't have it?"

I was scared and ashamed of what I had done and I did not want anyone to find out. I decided that Eric was right and getting rid of it was the best thing for everyone's sake.

Eric booked the appointment and dropped me off on the day but he did not stay. There were loads of young girls just like me at the clinic. Some of them had someone accompanying them, many others were alone but ultimately we were all there to destroy a life. I followed the nurse into a room where I had to get undressed and got prepared for the operation.

When the anesthesia wore off, I remember the doctors telling me that everything had gone well and I could go home later on that day. I looked down at my belly, my baby was gone, I felt so empty. I burst into tears and began crying uncontrollably.

The nurse just stared at me, "You've got what you wanted so why are you crying?"

I felt so awful, what type of person murders their own baby? Several days afterwards I was in tremendous pain. I experienced really sharp excruciating cramps, it was so severe that at one point I was sure that I was dying. I read the aftercare instructions I received from the clinic and it said that mild cramps for three days was normal but this pain was extreme. I had no one to turn to, therefore I suffered in silence. I locked myself away in my room and withdrew myself from the rest of the family to avoid answering any questions.

Months later I was still hurting, it was not as frequent as it was in the beginning but I was in agony when the abdominal cramps hit me. Consequently I went to visit the doctor and tests showed that I had an infection in my womb and tubes and as a result it had developed into Pelvic Inflammatory Disease. I was given antibiotics and it was treated but, despite that, it came back several months later. The lining of my fallopian tubes swelled up and the canals became much narrower. The doctor told me that because my body had been through so many complications at such a tender age, chances of me becoming pregnant in the future were highly unlikely.

I was heart-broken, I loved children and the thought of not being able to carry my own child again was unbearable. I felt like I was being punished for sleeping with Eric but if he hadn't touched me I would never ever have slept with him. I resented Nayla because she always had him around the house. Eric made sure that whenever no one was looking, he made a point of reminding me how much everyone would hate me if our dirty little secret ever got out. I loathed him for what he had done to me but I couldn't tell a soul given that I was also at fault. I felt trapped with no one to reach out to for support.

When Nayla dropped the bombshell that Eric wanted her to marry him, Mama and Daddy were so happy but I begged her not to marry him.

"Please don't say yes to him Nayla."

"Don't be silly sis, I love him, why would you even say such a thing?"

I looked for all the excuses in the world knowing I

sounded stupid but I could hardly tell her the real reason. Mama and Daddy found it amusing and thought it was cute that I did not want to lose my big sister to a guy.

"Nayla will always be your big sister regardless of who she marries."

"That's right, Pumpkin," Daddy said, in agreement with Mama.

Then Nayla chipped in, "Yeah babes I'm always going to be your sis and Eric will be like a big brother to you."

They spoke to me like I was a little child but I had been through more shit at fourteen than most grown-ups ever had to endure in their lifetime. I couldn't tell them so I had to sit back and watch Nayla marry Eric. She loved the monster who forced me to kill my baby. In a way I hated her for bringing him into our home in the first place.

Now that I had received a second chance to experience motherhood, I was not going to destroy my blessing. There was no way on earth that I would get rid of this baby. It did not matter how many threats Stephen made. This was my baby and abortion was not an option.

CHAPTER 14

I finally gathered the courage I needed to go and see Mama. I was too scared to call beforehand so I just showed up unexpectedly at the house. I could smell her cooking from outside, it smelled so delicious and reminded me just how much I missed her food. I took a deep breath and rang the doorbell.

"Who is it?" Mama called out.

"It's me Mama," I answered, sheepishly.

"Assariyah, is that really you?" she asked, fidgeting around with the locks.

"Yeah Mama it's me," I replied.

The door swung open and Mama was standing there. She looked so beautiful with her glowing cinnamon complexion and berry lips. She threw her arms around me, giving me a really tight hug, I hugged her back. I felt so good being wrapped up in Mama's embrace once more.

"I have missed you so much baby," she said, stroking my hair and kissing my cheeks.

"I've missed you too, Ma."

Snapping abruptly she pushed me away and landed a huge slap across my face.

"Where the hell have you been Assariyah? Do you have any idea what you have put me through for the past year? I have been worried sick about you and you didn't even have the decency to let me know that you were okay. Not even a single phone call from you Assariyah."

"I know Mama and I'm so sorry for not calling but I was too ashamed to face you after what happened at the wedding."

"That's the problem with you, you are always too busy thinking about yourself and too selfish to take anyone else's feelings into consideration. You know I am all by myself. Thank God for Nayla, otherwise I don't know where I would be."

"I'm sorry Ma."

She raised her hand, "Just stop! Sorry, sorry, sorry that is all I ever hear coming out of your mouth."

"Ma, I admit I was wrong for the way I handled things but you cannot make me feel any worse than I already do. I did not come here for a lecture so I guess I'll come back another time."

"Yes go ahead Assariyah, do what you do best, run away when the going gets tough. Let me tell you something though you cannot keep on running forever. Eventually things finally catch up with you and overflow. So go if you want to but the problem still remains."

She was right, I had to deal with this now or it would

only get harder. I followed her into the kitchen and prepared myself for the heat. I sat still and watched Mama as she poured a bag of white rice into the tomato sauce that was on the cooker, anticipating what she would say next.

"So where have you been hiding all this time Assariyah?"

"I haven't been hiding Ma, I just needed some time to sort things out and work out what I really want from life."

She stopped stirring the rice and diverted her attention back to me.

"And what have you figured out Assariyah?"

I didn't have an answer so remained silent.

"You know Cameron came here looking for you."

"He did, when?" I asked, totally stunned.

"About six weeks after the wedding. He mentioned something about you stopping by his place and him being too hard on you. He assumed that you would be staying here and wanted to talk. I tried calling your phone but it was disconnected and you never called home so I had no way of contacting you."

Her words struck a chord in my heart, my eyes filled up with tears. Oh my God, Cam came to see me, he wanted to talk but I was so busy running that I ended up running away from the one person that I really wanted to be with. He still loved me, maybe he was willing to give me a second chance and make things work.

I couldn't stop the tears from falling.

"There is no need crying over spilt milk Assariyah.

The truth is that man loved you dearly and you could have had it all, if you never sweated it all. Now please set the table for dinner."

I didn't blame Ma for being hard on me. She was never one to mince her words but I couldn't help but think of how different my life could have been with Cam. I knew for sure that I would never have got caught up in the whole escort game. I could have avoided all the drama and pain I had been through but she was right, thinking shoulda, coulda, woulda was pointless now. It was far too late. I was pregnant with another man's child. I just had to live with the fact that I'd never find out what Cameron wanted to say to me.

I laid the table just like Ma taught me to when I was younger. Her voice filled my head, 'Start from the outside and work your way in'. Poor table etiquette was one of her many pet peeves. Everything had to be set out perfectly, forks on the left, knives and spoons on the right and so on and so on.

Ma inspected the table, "It's nice to see you remembered some of the values I taught you." She dished us both a plate of Jollof rice with chicken and said grace before we tucked in.

Halfway into our meal, Mama put her fork down and grabbed my hand.

"I could sit here and tell you how embarrassed and ashamed your actions made me. For a long time I questioned my parenting skills, I felt maybe I failed you as a mother after your daddy died but Nayla turned out okay and I treated you both the same."

"No Ma, you didn't fail me as a mother."

"With a little help, I finally realised that this was not about me or how I felt but about you and your inner demons. Please help me understand why, Assariyah, so we can move on in peace."

I could tell that it was going to be a long evening and unless I gave Mama an explanation I wouldn't be leaving anytime soon. I hated delving back into the past but that is where it all stemmed from. My experiences with Eric had tainted my views on men and commitment. I cheated as a defence mechanism, that way if they cheated on me, it wouldn't hurt so bad.

I knew from an early age that I wanted financial security. Growing up I watched my daddy work his butt off, twelve hour shifts, six days a week just to keep a roof over our heads.

I asked him once, "Why do you work so much, Daddy?"

He replied, "I have to work hard, Pumpkin, to buy you, your sister and Ma nice things. That's what real men do, they take care of their family."

Daddy worked so hard that his work eventually killed him. He was working late on the railway tracks when he lost his balance and fell onto a live rail. There was nothing anyone could do to stop him being electrocuted. I was only sixteen when my daddy got stolen from me. It was my worst nightmare and I found it extremely hard to cope with, we all did. Ma had to take on Daddy's role as the provider. She worked like crazy, doing whatever jobs she could find, from cleaning, to cooking to tutoring our neighbours' children just to pay the bills but it was still not enough. I didn't want to live my life like that, so I chased money.

I couldn't tell Ma all of that without upsetting her further so I told her what she could handle. "I was wrong but I was scared of being poor Ma. I was so determined to get rich that I got caught up in the size of people's bank accounts rather than who they were as a person and, at first, I didn't care who got hurt."

She shook her head, "Well as you found out, marrying for money only ends in tears. Love is the only reason to ever get married Assariyah."

"I did love him Ma but by the time I realised that, the damage was already done."

She kissed my forehead, "I'm feeling a little tired so I'm going to take a nap. I hope you'll still be here when I wake up."

While Ma was sleeping I took the opportunity to look through our old family pictures. I experienced every type of emotion you could think of. At first there was joy at seeing all four of us together but I felt sorrowful that Daddy was no longer with us. Then I cringed at the horrific sight of me in those matching floral dresses and ribbons that Mama used to make me wear to church. I missed the way we were though.

After I exhausted our family albums, I picked up the copy of Pride Magazine that was laying on the solid mahogany coffee table in the living room. I used to be a regular subscriber to the magazine but hadn't read one for ages and was excited to see what was new. As I flicked through I spotted a few items that I liked and made a note of where I could purchase them from. The magazine featured an article on the top twenty black power couples in the UK and focused on how they managed to balance work and married life. I remember thinking how great it was to see so many black people doing their thing and I was filled with a sense of pride.

However, when I came across couple number five, my eyes popped out my head in horror. The headline stated, 'With a staggering £50 million between them, it is no surprise that Politician Stephen Richards and his beautiful wife, Doctor Jasmina Richards, are #5 on our list!' No fucking way, I said out loud as I stared at the images of Stephen and Jasmina together. Power couple my ass, they were more like the poisonous devil couple.

The two people I hated the most were living under the same roof. They had fucked me over and it was pay-back time. It infuriated me to think that, in the space of a year, Jasmina had got married after destroying my fairytale wedding. She had gotten away from me one too many times but this time I was determined that there would be no escape. They would both pay for hurting me.

I left Ma a note telling her something came up so I had to leave. I left ten thousand pounds in cash for her and jotted down my number for her to contact me. I ripped out the article of the Richards and stuffed it inside my Birkin bag and left the family house. The madness was about to begin.

CHAPTER 15

Revenge was all I could think about. It was so close, I could smell it and I couldn't wait to taste its sweet aroma. Yes, they would pay for everything that they had done to me. The look on Jasmina's face would be absolutely priceless when it came to light that her husband had tasted my pussy juices and had planted his seed inside me. It was her turn to experience what it felt like to have your whole world turned upside down in the blink of an eye. I had to think of a plan and execute it perfectly. There was no room for error, God knows that I had waited too long for this moment to fuck it all up now.

I searched through my camera and prayed that it still had the footage of Stephen and I having sex with each other back in Miami. I pressed play and hoped for the best. Bingo! It was still there. Thank God I hadn't deleted it as planned. It was time to get things moving. I uploaded the content onto my laptop and made a few hard copies for safe measure.

Once that was done I attached a note with the DVD.

Dear Mr & Mrs Richards,

Please find enclosed a DVD for your viewing pleasure. I want £5 million by Friday. If you fail to deliver I'm sure that the News of the World will have a field day watching MP Stephen Richards in action. I trust that you would both like to avoid the public embarrassment so make sure you have £5 million in cash ready for me by Friday. Call me on 07794921129 to finalise the details.

Assariyah
aka
Rose Monet

I didn't have their home address so I had no other choice but to send it by recorded delivery to the hospital where Jasmina worked. I felt satisfied knowing that in a couple of days Jasmina would finally get what she deserved. The best part about it all was the fact that she wouldn't even know what had hit her. As for Stephen, he wanted me to kill my baby and he was sleeping with the enemy, therefore he was going to pay too.

The icing on the cake was that I would be five million pounds richer. Wow, five mill to my name. Life would be a dream. The first thing I planned to do with the money was to give one million to my mum. That way she would be more than comfortable for retirement and my mind would be at ease even if I was halfway across the world.

I couldn't stay in London, there was nothing but bad

memories left for me here. I needed a fresh start and Miami was calling my name. Moving abroad would allow me to raise my baby in peace and, once I picked up this money, my baby would be set for life. There was no way in hell that my child would ever want for anything or go through the things I went through. All I had to do was wait for either Jasmina or Stephen to call. The suspense was playing heavily on my mind and made me restless.

The next day I received a call from Jasmina. She approached me in a very short and direct manner. "Assariyah I received your package. Meet me at 103 Ridgway Road in Wimbledon at 8pm on Friday." The phone went down before I could even say a word. There was no emotion in Jasmina's voice which threw me off slightly. I was prepared for her to be angry or upset but she was emotionless and that worried me. I couldn't tap into her thoughts and that made me feel uneasy. There was a time we were best friends who finished each other's sentences off and now we were complete strangers. She had taken everything away from me and I hated her with every bone in my body. It's funny how thin the line between love and hate really is. As far as I was concerned, Friday could not come any sooner.

CHAPTER 16

My heart was racing as I approached the Richards' door. With sweaty palms I rang the doorbell and waited nervously. Jasmina opened the door wearing a white jumpsuit, her hair was pulled back in a ponytail.

"Going somewhere?" I asked. She stared me down for a minute or so before stepping aside to let me in. I followed her into the kitchen.

"Assariyah Jones ends up as nothing more than a common prostitute, who would ever have thought it?" she said in a sardonic tone.

"Well your husband sure loves common, he had no complaints," I fired back at her.

"Aaah yes my husband, how could I forget…"

I cut her off before she could finish her sentence, "Let's skip the small talk Jasmina, I really haven't got time for this shit. Just give me the money and I'm out of here."

"What's the rush Assariyah? Relax you'll get the money. Sit down and have a drink with me first."

She poured a glass of red wine. I waved my hand,

"No not for me thanks."

"Oh silly me, I almost forgot. We've got some juice fruit punch, I'll get you that instead."

"You really don't have to worry."

"It's no bother, I insist," she said, walking over to the double door refrigerator. She poured me some juice.

"Let's make a toast," she raised her glass. "Here is to you being five million pounds richer." Jasmina sipped her wine and I followed suit, taking a sip of the fruit punch.

Jasmina smirked, "I'll be right back."

A few minutes went by before she came back into the kitchen holding two big black holdall bags. She handed them over to me. I opened the bags and they were both filled to the brim with bank notes. I smiled internally, knowing that all my dreams were just a stone throw away.

"It's all in there," Jasmina said. She picked up her glass before downing it in one go, "Drink up."

I finished my fruit punch and grabbed the bags. The bags were extremely heavy but I was determined not to put them down until I got home. Money always gave me strength.

"I trust that we no longer have to worry about the matter at hand becoming public now that you have your money," Jasmina said. I reassured her that they had kept their side of the deal and so would I.

"Good, now take the money and get your miscarriaging self out of my house."

I was horrified and instinctively reached for my belly, dropping everything I was holding except from my handbag.

"What the hell is that supposed to mean?" I asked her in a state of panic.

"See Assariyah, your problem is that you always underestimated me. You may be more beautiful than I am but you'll never be smarter than me. I thought you would have learnt that I'm always ten steps ahead of you after what happened on your wedding day with Cameron."

"Leave Cam out of this," I warned her.

"Did you really think that I was going to sit back and let you live happily ever after, raising my husband's first child?"

"What are you talking about?"

She ignored me and carried on with her speech. "Hahahaha clearly you've read far too much fucking fairytales, watched too many Hollywood movies. Look at you, even now you thought you could just barge into my home with your bull and what everything would go your way. You expected me to hand you five million of our hard earned money just like that."

"Quit talking in riddles, what the fuck are you going on about Jasmina?"

"I haven't even carried a child for my husband and I'll be damned if another woman, especially a tramp whore like you, carries my husband's first born."

"As you know I'm already pregnant and there is nothing you or anyone can do to stop me from having this baby."

I gathered my things and was about to leave when she shouted out at me. "Wrong, tonight you will be in extreme pain. That baby in your womb will fall out in blood clots."

"God forbid," I yelled out.

"Save your useless prayers, that drink you just drank was laced with Mifeprex," she sneered.

"Mife…mif…mife what?" I stuttered, unable to get my words out.

"Mifeprex, I wouldn't expect your dumb ass to understand but the process has already started. Your uterine lining is probably shedding as we speak."

"Oh my God, nooooooooooo, my baby, I need to get to the hospital now."

"It's too late, trust me I'm a doctor," Jasmina said, throwing me a bottle. "There are four tablets of Misoprostol in there. You have between the next 24-72 hours to take them."

Everything she was saying to me sounded so foreign. All I could think about was my unborn child. I could not lose this baby, I just couldn't.

"I would have given it to you all at once but I thought it was only fair that you had the final control over the timing your pregnancy expels."

"Nooooooooooooo," I cried out in agony with tears flooding down my cheeks. "You are one evil bitch. How could you do this?" I asked clasping my belly.

Jasmina just stood there laughing like nothing mattered.

"How could you kill an innocent baby?"

Her laughter grew even louder. The witch had taken this shit one step too far. Not my baby, that was the one good thing I had left to look forward to. The baby was my second chance at life and she had stolen another piece of my happiness from me. I only wanted the money to start afresh and build a new life. I didn't want my baby to ever go through the shit I went through. I was so hungry for money that I was willing to get it by any means necessary, but this is not what I wanted. My pursuit for money had cost me everything. I had nothing left to live for.

Everything went black. I was shaking and trembling involuntarily, I remember reaching inside my bag and pulling out the Snubnose .38 special I always carried with me. Aiming right in between her eyes I pulled the trigger. The bitch had killed my baby so she had to die. I emptied five rounds into her head before turning the gun on myself. I pulled the trigger, the gun clicked. Nothing happened, I was out of bullets. It was over in about five seconds or less, it all happened so quickly.

I was in a state of shock, I didn't even notice when Stephen entered the kitchen. Rocking Jasmina's lifeless body in his arms, he wailed, "What have you done?" There was blood everywhere. The white shirt Stephen was wearing had turned red. I couldn't believe that I had actually killed her.

I heard the police sirens and knew they were coming to take me away. I wanted them to kill me. My baby was gone, I had nothing to live for.

CHAPTER 17

Within minutes sirens and flashing lights flooded the streets. The police, paramedics and news-reporting crews surrounded the Richards' home, along with several of their horrified neighbours. Two of the police officers read me my rights and cuffed me.

As they lead me into their vehicle, the reporters shouted out, "Why did you do it?" "What made you kill her?" To my relief, the blue tape the police had put up stopped them from getting any closer to me.

Back at the police station I was asked if I wanted a duty solicitor and I accepted the offer. The severity of the case was more than I could handle, I was in deep and needed help. When the duty solicitor arrived I was taken into a small room.

"Hi I'm Siobhan Givens," she said, pushing up her glasses. "I need you to tell me exactly what happened tonight step by step."

I was pretty shaken up but managed to tell her everything.

"What is going to happen to me?" I asked anxiously.

"There is no way to sugar coat this Miss Jones, you are facing between twenty to thirty years."

"Twenty to thirty years, I'm as good as dead. I won't survive in prison. Please you've got to help me."

"I'm afraid that is the minimum sentence you are looking at for the crime you committed."

I was doomed, I didn't even know why I agreed to have a duty solicitor. Everybody knew that duty solicitors were a load of shit. They didn't give a fuck what happened to me, they worked for the system. The bitch just reinforced that with the crap she was throwing my way. So when the time came for the police to interview me I decided to remain silent.

"It will be in your best interest to tell us what happened," one of the officers said.

I replied, "No comment." In the end they finally gave up trying to interview me on that night and threw me back in the cell.

Throughout the night I was in intense pain, I experienced really bad cramps and I could feel the blood in between my legs. I was devastated, I felt my baby dying and there was nothing I could do to save him or her. I cried out for help but the pigs just banged on the cell doors and kept telling me to shut up.

It was only in the morning when one of the officers found me sprawled out on the floor with blood in between my legs that I was rushed to the hospital. I was exhausted and the cramping only got worse. Tests showed that I had heavy doses of Mifeprex in my blood. Even though I hadn't taken any Misprostol, the levels of

Mifeprex in my body had caused me to have a complete miscarriage.

The doctors advised the police that, under the circumstances, it was best for them to keep me in the hospital overnight. I was handcuffed to the hospital bed, with two officers guarding the room. The shorter of the two officers walked into my room holding a Krispy Kreme doughnut in one hand and *The Sun* newspaper in the other.

He held it up high, "Look you made front page news," he said pointing to the headlines. *'Wife of MP Stephen Richards Murdered In Cold Blood By Jealous Ex-Best Friend Assariyah Jones.'*

He threatened, "You're going to have to start speaking soon or chances of your pretty face seeing the light of day again are finished."

I closed my eyes and thought of Mama, this would destroy her.

I still hadn't exercised my right to make a phone call so once I got back to the police station that was the first thing I asked for. I dialled Mama's number, she broke down crying at the sound of my voice.

"Assariyah what have you done? You are all over the news. Please tell me it's not true."

"I'm sorry Mama I don't have long to explain but I need your help. I need a really good solicitor."

"I called Cameron earlier this morning."

"You did what?"

"I didn't know what else to do. He told me that he would get you a good solicitor."

"He did, well okay I'm being held at Wimbledon, I'm

so scared tell him to hurry please Mama. Thanks, I love you."

"I love you too."

I was shocked that Cameron was still willing to help me after everything I had put him through, but more than anything I was grateful for his help. Lord knows that without a good lawyer, I would have spent the best years of my life rotting away in a jail cell.

Being the good man that he was, Cameron was true to his word. He got me one of the best lawyers in the UK, Barry Grant, who studied at Oxford University and was renowned for a ninety nine percent success rate. After several strenuous months of fighting my case, he managed to get me off on a lesser charge of voluntary manslaughter. He argued that I was provoked by Jasmina, who abused her position as a doctor. He presented her as a jealous and angry wife who resented the fact that her husband had an affair and impregnated another woman, thus poisoning me and unlawfully aborting my baby.

The judge sentenced me to seven to ten years in prison, which was still a long time for me but it was a lot better than the original twenty to thirty years I was looking at. I can only describe my time in Holloway as hell. Locked up in a cell infested by cockroaches, repeating the same procedures over and over again. Every day was the same, the sound of the guards' footsteps, rattling keys and heavy metal doors slamming. Women screaming all night out of desperation, wanting to escape the inhumane conditions we were confined to.

It was too much for some of the women, many

suffered from mental health issues and would often self-harm. It is still very difficult for me to digest the images of people wrapping tissue around their body and setting themselves on fire. Unfortunately, in the end, after several bids, many finally succeeded with their suicide attempts.

As sad as it was I tried not to allow myself to dwell on those things. Only the strong survived behind these walls. I had to learn to block a lot of things out of my mind. I found that meditating helped me a great deal with handling the stress, well it has helped me maintain my sanity so far.

I was fortunate enough to receive support from the outside world, some of the others were not so lucky. They received no mail and no visitation, imagine how lonely life is for them. Although Mama didn't come to visit me, she wrote to me all the time. She came to see me once but it was too unbearable for her so she put her feelings down on paper instead. Cameron wrote to me throughout my trial and, even when it was over, the letters still kept coming. He even came to see me about once every six weeks. I appreciated Cameron for sticking by me even after the way I treated him. He was heaven sent and that only makes me regret the fact that I took our relationship for granted even more.

For most of the time, it felt great to see a friendly face. At other times it made me miss the outside world even more than I already did. Two and a half years had passed and his loyalty and support remained priceless but things were about to change.

This time round when Cameron came to see me he

told me that it would be his last ever visit. "Assariyah I'm getting married soon and my wife to be is not comfortable with my appearances here." His words pierced a hole through my heart. He hadn't mentioned anything about being in a relationship so it was totally unexpected.

"But I need you Cam," I cried.

"I'm sorry Assariyah but I've gotta go now. I've done all that I can for you. Take care of yourself, okay."

He gave me a hug then kissed my forehead the same way he used to all those years ago.

"Thank you for everything Cameron," I struggled to choke out.

He waved and as I watched Cameron walk out my life for good, a part of me died when he disappeared through those doors. There were a million and one things I would do differently if I could start my life from scratch. Way back then it was supposed to be me and him, I should have been his wife, not her.

I sat in my cell crying, Mama's words haunted me, she was right. I could have had it all, if I never sweated it all.